The Faces of Fantasy

Also by Patti Perret

THE FACES OF SCIENCE FICTION

The Faces of Fantasy

Photographs by Patti Perret

Introduction by Terri Windling

TOR®

A TOM DOHERTY ASSOCIATES BOOK

NEW YORK

THE FACES OF FANTASY

Copyright © 1996 by Patti Perret

This book is printed on acid-free paper.

Cover design by Kristin Johnson

Edited by James Frenkel

A Tor Book
Published by Tom Doherty Associates, Inc.
175 Fifth Avenue
New York, NY 10010

Tor Books on the World Wide Web:
http://www.tor.com

Tor® is a registered trademark of Tom Doherty Associates, Inc.

Library of Congress Cataloging-in-Publication Data

Perret, Patti, date
    The faces of fantasy / Patti Perret. —1st ed.
        p.   cm.
    "A Tom Doherty Associates book."
    ISBN 0–312–86182–6 (hardcover) (acid-free paper)
    ISBN 0–312–86216–4 (paper) (acid-free paper)
    1. Authors, American—20th century—Portraits. 2. Fantastic fiction—Authorship.
    3. Authors, English—20th century—Portraits. 4. Portrait photography.
    I. Title.
    PS374.F27P47   1996
    813'.0876609—dc20
    [B]   96–18276

First edition: October 1996

Printed in England

0 9 8 7 6 5 4 3 2 1

The publisher would like to thank the following parties for their help and cooperation in the gathering of photographs for use in the Introduction:

Culver Pictures, Inc., for permission to reprint photographs of the following subjects:
  Beauty and the Beast, directed by Jean Cocteau (1946)
  Hans Christian Andersen
  Edgar Rice Burroughs
  Lewis Carroll
  Lord Dunsany
  William Morris
  Christina Rossetti
  theatrical production of *A Midsummer Night's Dream,* by William Shakespeare
  Alfred, Lord Tennyson
  Oscar Wilde
  William Butler Yeats;

HarperCollins*Publishers* (U.K.), for permission to reprint the photograph of J. R. R. Tolkien, by John Wyatt;

Patti Perret, for permission to reprint the photographs of Mask, by Wendy Froud, and of Fritz Leiber.

For
Mark, Shannon, and Riley,
who continue to give me a wider vision of the world

Acknowledgments

First and foremost I wish to thank the writers for putting a part of themselves into this project and for giving of their precious time. It's been an honor for me to work with you all.

Betsy Wollheim has been there from the start of this project, and seen me through to the finish. Her support, advice, encouragement, and friendship have been instrumental in making this book happen.

Thanks to James Frenkel, my editor, whose dedication and enthusiasm for this project allowed me to continue doing this work; to Tom Doherty for publishing this book; to Jim Minz for his helpful assistance; and to all the folks at Tor who helped make the book I envisioned.

Many friends have been supportive and helpful throughout this extended project. I am very grateful to Kristin Johnson for her creative input and encouragement; Kathy Kennedy at Photo Works for her help and advice; Elsie Wollheim, whose spirit will never leave me; Susan Scofield for all her help and fun traveling in England and Ireland; and to Brian Cullman for introducing me to the work of so many great writers.

One of the great pleasures of making this book was to visit with friends in faraway places. Many thanks go to: Adele Baker, Dan Bonnell and Lea Floden, Arden Bucklin, Nora and Kathy Connors, Melanie Hedlund, Nate Herman and Ginny Meredith, Mabel McLoughlin, John Morthland, Karen Moscowitz, Gloria Norris, Lisa Levitt Ryckman, John Scofield, Dale Sophia and Elania Nanopoulos, Nanci Reese, Peter Stampfel, Rich Stim and Angel C. C., Mary Virginia Swanson, Jackie and Christoph Waltz.

Traveling for work and raising a family are not real easy, but I had the best help in the world from my parents, Alma and Clifford Perret, and my in-laws, Marian and Ed Perregaux. I don't know what I would have done without you. Most especially thanks to my partner in life, Mark Bingham, for your love and support.

Terri Windling

ONCE UPON A TIME a seed was planted in the fertile loam of language and Earth. The seed sprouted, unfurling tales like leaves: the first stories ever told. The seedling drank down rain and sun and grew, in time, into a mighty tree, holding the earth together in its knotted roots, the sky in its arms. The Tree of Story is as old as time—twin to the mythic Tree of Life whose image appears on Sumerian artifacts of Mesopotamia (c. 4000–3500 B.C.)—and among the earliest artworks of most cultures around the globe. The Norse conceived of the universe as a huge ash tree called Yggdrasil, linking the worlds of man and the gods, roots reaching down to the lands of the dead. The Celts created a Tree Alphabet; the African Ibo endowed them with souls; the Greeks heard prophecies in the rustling leaves of the autumn oak.

The Tree of Story is rooted in such mythic lore from the ancient world. Its trunk contains sagas, epics, romances, fables, fairy tales, and folktales. It has grown tall through the centuries, with many limbs and countless leaves, nurtured not only by the elements but by sheer human inventiveness: by the creation of our alphabet, cheap paper, ink, and movable type; by literacy, technology, and mass book distribution. On this Tree of Story, literature itself is a relatively recent growth compared to the performance arts and to oral storytelling. Within the literary arts, fantasy is a sturdy limb—not separate from the rest of literature, as modern critics (and bookstore categorizations) often suggest. It is a limb both older and stronger than the average reader might realize; and yet, despite its age, it continues to produce fresh shoots, fresh leaves, fresh stories.

Our earliest tales were magical ones. Just think of those that have survived the centuries: Mesopotamia's *Gilgamesh,*

Mask, by Wendy Froud

Alfred, Lord Tennyson

Homer's Greek *Odyssey,* the Icelandic *Eddas,* the Germanic *Niebulunglied, The Epic of the Cid* from Spain, the *Charlemagne* cycle from France, the *Volsunga Saga* from Finland, *The Mabinogion* from Wales, *The Tain* from Ireland, *Beowulf* and the whole *Matter of Britain* . . . all tales of quests, riddles, spells, and transformations; all part of the trunk of the tree that supports Western literature today. Such epic stories were privileged ones, coming to us in written form. The rest were passed from mouth to mouth in preliterate societies, often in the guise we call Mother Goose, old wives' or fairy tales.

Mythology has been woven through our literary arts for hundreds of years—particularly the classical myths of Greece and Rome, Judeo-Christian legendry, and the mix of Celtic and Norman tales that make up the Arthurian cycle. Writers of the past were unashamed to use myths, dreams, and flights of fantasia as potent raw material for the storyteller's art. Virgil's *Aeneid,* Ovid's *Metamorphoses,* Dante's *Divine Comedy,* Milton's *Paradise Lost,* Blake's *Songs of Innocence* and *Songs of Experience,* Morris's *Defense of Guinevere,* Tennyson's *Idylls of the King* . . . these are but a few of the works richly steeped in legendry that have inspired writers in our own century—writers like John Barth (*Chimera*), John Gardner (*Grendel*), Robert Nye (*Merlin*), A. A. Attanasio (*The Dragon and the Unicorn*), Roberto Calasso (*The Marriage of Cadmus and Harmony*), Ursule Molinaro (*The New Moon with the Old Moon in Her Arms*), James Morrow (*Towing Jehovah*), James P. Blaylock (*The Paper Grail*), and Robert Holdstock (*Mythago Wood*), all of whom have written modern mythic novels that work with timeless themes.

William Morris

All but the last three of these books were published as mainstream fiction, and the latter three (published as fantasy) would be equally at home on the mainstream shelves. Historically, American literature has had an almost puritanical bias in favor of strict realism—one that is slightly less stringent in England, and gloriously absent in Latin America and other parts of the world where the most vital contemporary fiction can be found. Nonetheless even in America mythology remains an acceptable subject for the serious author to contemplate—a respectability enhanced by excellent nonfiction on the subject by the likes of Robert Graves (*The White Goddess*) and Joseph Campbell (*The Hero with a Thousand Faces, The Masks of God,* et cetera).

By contrast, folklore and fairy tales are the poor country cousins of mythology. Folktales don't concern the gods and the broad workings of the universe—they are tales about human men and women, told with deceptive simplicity; stories of transformation and survival: of children abandoned in the woods, daughters handed poisoned apples and sons setting off on perilous roads, men and women struck down by wolves or imprisoned in enchanters' towers. Such tales have survived for thousands of years because they speak of timeless concerns: fear, courage, greed, generosity, cruelty, compassion, failure, and triumph. Fairy and folktales use archetypes as a mirror held up to daily life, particularly the lives of those without clear avenues of social power (women, children, social outcasts, and peasants). Without the cachet of mythic fiction, stories rooted in folktale themes are more likely to find themselves relegated to the genre shelves. In the last two decades, as a result, fine authors orphaned by the literary mainstream due to an unfashionable interest in folklore and "post-realism" (to use a term current among young writers) have found a home in the fantasy field or in the field of children's fiction—making these two of the liveliest areas of book publishing today.

Our culture's pairing of fantasy and children dates back only to Victorian England, but to understand it we must go farther back to the sixteenth and seventeenth centuries. Although some historians will disagree, this is where I like to think the modern fantasy field began: when deterministically magical tales (inspired by the oral folk tradition) were composed by literary writers of the day and published for an adult readership. Giovanni Francesco Straparola's bawdy collection *The Delectable Nights* was published in Venice in 1550, influencing the work of the Neopolitan writer Giambattista Basile, whose *Il Pentamerone: The Tale of Tales,* a cycle of fifty enchanted stories, was published early in the next century. These Italian tales would certainly have been known by Jeanne L'Heritier de Villadon, Marie-Catherine d'Aulnoy, Madame Leprince de Beaumont, Charles Perrault, and other habitués of the French literary salons who created their own adult fairy tales, publishing them to great acclaim throughout the seventeenth century. (These stories were eventually collected in the *Cabinet des Fées.*)

Such literary fairy tales (and the older oral tales they drew upon) were rich, complex, and sensual works never meant for children's ears. Straparola had to defend his book against charges of indecency before the Venetian Inquisition; Basile's "Sleeping Beauty" (one of the earliest extant versions of the story), is wakened not by a chaste, respectful kiss, but by the birth of twins after the prince has come, fornicated with the sleeping body, and left again. The French stories were less exuberantly scatological than the Italian ones, but were nonetheless written for an audience presumed to be adult, aristocratic, and educated. It was in the French salons that the term "fairy tale" ("*conte de fée*") was coined—a colorful but misleading label, as many of the stories falling under it do not contain creatures called fairies at all. Rather, they are wonder tales, or märchen (to use the German word)—tales about ordinary men and women in a world invested with magic.

Beauty and the Beast

Although Charles Perrault is the name history has singled out from this prolific group, he was by no means the most influential or widely read among his *conte de fée* peers. The majority of the works collected and published in the forty-one volumes of the *Cabinet des Fées* were written by women writers who were quite successful in their day—such as Madame de Villeneuve, author of

17

the original *Beauty and the Beast,* and Madame D'Aulnoy, author of *The Green Snake, The White Deer,* and many others. These were educated women with an unusual degree of artistic independence, and within their use of the fantasy form one can find distinctly subversive subtext.

A Midsummer Night's Dream

That these women should be drawn to material from the oral tradition is not surprising, for the folk story, like so many anonymous arts, has historically been a female preserve. As Alison Lurie has pointed out (in *Once upon a Time*), "throughout Europe (except in Ireland), the storytellers from whom the Grimm brothers and their followers collected their material were most often women; in some areas they were all women. For hundreds of years, while written literature was almost exclusively the province of men, these tales were being invented and passed on orally by women." Straparola, in his defense to the Venetian Inquisition, stated he had

Christina Rossetti

merely written down stories told to him by a circle of female acquaintances; Basile, too, acknowledged drawing his inspiration from women's tales. Hundreds of years later, educated, ambitious women like those in the French salons continue to be drawn to themes that lie beneath the surface of old folktales, using their metaphoric language in interesting, occasionally subversive ways. You will see, flipping through the pages of this book, that modern fantasy fiction is one area of the literary arts where women are well represented, once again.

In England, medieval fairy tales were an influence on two major writers: poet Edmund Spenser, author of *The Faerie Queene,* and playwright William Shakespeare, whose *Tempest* and

William Butler Yeats

Midsummer Night's Dream drew from English and European lore. In Germany, the French *Cabinet de Fées*—published in the eighteenth century—had a profound effect (along with the new field of German folktale collection) on the works of German Romantics like Novalis, Ludwig Tieck, E. T. A. Hoffmann, and Johann Wolfgang von Goethe. By the nineteenth century, England, too, had developed a passion for folktale collection, and these folktales found their way, in turn, into the fiction and poetry of the day, such as George Macdonald's *Phantastes* and *Lilith,* John Ruskin's *King of the Golden River,* Christina Rossetti's *Goblin Market,* Rudyard Kipling's *Puck of Pook's Hill,* the fairy poetry of William Butler Yeats, and the fairy tales of Oscar Wilde. The pre-Raphaelite artist/socialist/poet William Morris published *The Wood beyond the World,* set in a wholly imaginary land, carefully constructed and convincing, considered by many to be the first modern adult fantasy novel. H. Rider Haggard wrote mythic adventure novels like *King*

Oscar Wilde

Hans Christian Andersen

Lewis Carroll

Solomon's Mines; Lewis Carroll published his wonderful absurdist fantasy, *Alice in Wonderland;* and across the channel in Denmark, Hans Christian Andersen was penning those wise and wistful tales for which he is justly famed.

Despite the great popularity of these magical works, by the end of the century the pendulum of adult literary taste began, once again, to swing away from fantasy and the mystical medievalism popularized by the pre-Raphaelites. Magical tales were now too closely associated with previous generations—with old farmwives and everything rural, backward, and old-fashioned. The industrial revolution, rising literacy, and the sudden growth of a new middle class had created a booming publishing industry in which novels of social realism were the preferred literary form. Magical fiction, along with oral tales, was relegated to children's nurseries—rather like, J. R. R. Tolkien pointed out in his essay "On Fairy Stories," "shabby or old fashioned furniture . . . primarily because the adults do not want it, and do not mind if it is misused." The separate field of fiction for children was firmly established during these years. Chapbooks (and, later, gorgeously illustrated books) aimed specifically at young readers reprinted fairy tales from the *Cabinet des Fées* and other such cheap story sources—greatly simplifying them in the process, stripping them of ambiguity, sensuality, and subversiveness; turning fiesty heroes and heroines into models of Victorian behavior; and often publishing the tales with no author's name attached at all—as if these tales also were anonymous works from the oral folk tradition. (Regrettably, such altered versions of the tales are the ones we're most familiar with today, and fairy tales are now presumed to be children's stories only.)

Despite fantasy's fall from literary grace, magical work continued to be written, published, and read in the first half of our own century. Some authors found refuge in the children's book field—like Edith Nesbit, author of the *The Enchanted Castle;* J. M. Barrie, author of the immortal *Peter Pan;* and L. Frank Baum, creator of the Oz series. Some slipped fantasy stories in among other works for which they were better known—like E. M. Forster, author of quite a number of gently magical tales, and James Thurber, author of the delightful *The Thirteen Clocks.* The Irish, always iconoclastic, were unafraid to present overtly fantastic works—like James Stephen's fey novel *The Crock of Gold,* and the dreamlike tales of Lord Dunsany, author of the classic fantasy novel *The King of Elfland's Daughter.* Hannes Bok (author

Lord Dunsany

of *The Sorcerer's Ship*), Hope Mirrlees (author of *Lud-in-the-Mist*), and others produced unabashedly magical novels as the century progressed, but six English writers in particular published works that more than any others shaped the field for years to come: E. R. Eddison (a singular stylist, author of *The Worm Ouroboros* and the language-rich Zimiamvian trilogy); T. H. White (the author of the charming Arthurian classic, *The Once and Future King*); Mervyn Peake (author of the deliciously gothic Gormenghast trilogy); and the Inklings, three dons from Oxford who shared a love of theology, linguistics, and magical literature: Charles Williams (author of *The Greater Trumps* and other mystical adult novels); C. S. Lewis (noted critic, and author of the much-loved Narnia series for children); and J. R. R. Tolkien (the celebrated author of *The Hobbit* and *The Lord of the Rings*).

While all this was going on in England, in America fantasy was going down a very different road as a consequence of the success of pulp magazines in the middle of the century—particularly *Weird Tales* and *Unknown* magazines, the latter edited by the influential John W. Campbell alongside his magazine *Astounding Science-Fiction*. Thus while in England fantasy was becoming more and more associated with children's fiction, in America, because of the pulps, it was becoming associated with the young science fiction field. The pulp magazines specialized in "heroic fantasy," typified by the enormously popular Conan stories of Robert E. Howard, the "forgotten worlds" adventures of A. Merritt, and the Tarzan of the Apes jungle stories

J.R.R. Tolkien

of Edgar Rice Burroughs. The best of these fantasy adventure tales were colorful, fast-paced, witty, and written with tongue firmly in cheek by writers like Fritz Leiber (the Fafhrd and Gray Mouser series) and

Edgar Rice Burroughs

Fritz Leiber

L. Sprague de Camp (*The Goblin Tower* and, in collaboration with Fletcher Pratt, *The Land of Unreason*). The works of other important American fantasists began to appear about this time, among them the hauntingly magical contemporary tales of Ray Bradbury (*Something Wicked This Way Comes*), the masterful stories of Theodore Sturgeon (*E Pluribus Unicorn*), the great utopian fantasy of Austin Tappan Wright (*Islandia*), and the quirky, mythic fantasy of Thomas Burnett Swann (*The Day of the Minotaur*).

Although J. R. R. Tolkien's enormously influential trilogy, *The Lord of the Rings*, was first published in the 1950s, it did not reach a mass audience (particularly in the United States) until a decade later. In the early 1970s, taking note of Tolkien's devoted following, Ian and Betty Ballantine of Ballantine Books (two of the most inspired publishing figures in the fantasy field) launched the Sign of the Unicorn line of adult fantasy fiction. Edited by Lin Carter (who was himself a writer of heroic tales) and marketed with distinctive covers, many of them by the gently surrealist painter Gervasio Gallardo, this series brought works of classic literary fantasy into paperback, introducing a whole generation to authors like George Macdonald, William Morris, Lord Dunsany, E. R. Eddison, James Branch Cabell, Mervyn Peake, and many others—in addition to promoting new authors like Peter S. Beagle and Joy Chant. The series was not a runaway commercial success and thus proved to be short-lived, but its impact on the fantasy field was far greater than this might suggest. A whole new generation of writers cut their teeth on these classic works thanks to the Sign of the Unicorn line, courtesy of Mr. Carter. (Carter's nonfiction book, *Imaginary Worlds*, was the bible for young writers at the time.)

Subsequently, Judy-Lynn and Lester del Rey (the latter also a fantasy writer) founded the Del Rey fantasy line at Ballantine. They introduced readers to Terry Brooks (*The Sword of Shannara*) and Stephen R. Donaldson (the Thomas Covenant series), whose multivolume series books quickly hit the best-sellers lists. Thus the line was off to a running start (thanks in part to the marketing genius of Judy-Lynn del Rey), proving that there was indeed an audience for adult fantasy fiction. The Lin Carter and Del Rey lines mark the birth of the fantasy genre as we know it—and yet, as the 1970s waned, Del Rey Books was still the only American publisher with an adult fantasy imprint. Other houses published fantasy titles under a science fiction label—a system that made some sense at the time because the little fantasy available then was largely of the Howardian kind (i.e., similar to Howard's Conan tales, also known as "sword-and-sorcery"), which had grown, like American science fiction, out of the pulp magazines. Of these publishing houses, Donald A. and Elsie Wollheim's DAW Books (devoted to genre fiction) and Dell Books, which began a short-lived fantasy program in 1979, were the only ones that published more than the occasional fantasy title.

Ace Books, where I worked as an editor at the beginning of the 1980s, was the next publisher to create an adult fantasy imprint—albeit they did so rather warily, still afraid to commit money and rack space to this upstart genre. Much of what was in print in those days seemed to be aimed at adolescent boys, with covers sporting large-breasted women swooning at the feet of muscle-bound men. (Little wonder then that the literary establishment dismissed the genre as a whole.) High fantasy, à là Tolkien, was in seriously short supply—and so as an editor one had to find, encourage, and launch new authors in order to keep up with growing reader demand for this kind of fiction. Thus a large number of talented new writers came into the field all at once—writers of both genders, writing for a readership that was equally mixed. These writers, unlike the generation before, did not grow up with the pulp magazines; nor did they necessarily come from SF, with which fantasy has long been paired. They came from a variety of disciplines, with backgrounds in world literature and myth, Medieval and Renaissance history, Celtic folk music, oral storytelling, and other performance arts. Embracing the modern fantasy field in order to write folkloric tales and contemporary "magic realism," they traded literary respectability for an eager and informed readership.

Today, most major publishing houses boast successful fantasy lists, and annual sales of fantasy books exceed those of horror and SF. This relatively young genre is an untapped vein of gold within the landscape of modern fiction, containing some of the most beautifully written works of the late century by writers like Peter S. Beagle (*A Fine and Private Place*), Orson Scott Card (*Seventh Son*), Suzy McKee Charnas (*Dorothea Dreams*), Susan Cooper (*The Dark Is Rising*), John Crowley (*Little, Big*), Karen Joy Fowler (*Sarah Canary*), Mary Gentle (*Rats and Gargoyles*), Lisa Goldstein (*Tourists*), M. John Harrison (*The Course of the Heart*), Barry Hughart (*Eight Skilled Gentlemen*), Ellen Kushner (*Thomas the Rhymer*), Tanith Lee (*Forests of the Night*), Ursula K. Le Guin (*A Wizard of Earthsea*), Patricia A. McKillip (*The Book of Atrix Wolfe*), Robin McKinley (*The Door in the Hedge*), Michael Moorcock (*Gloriana*), Tim Powers (*The Anubis Gates*), Geoff Ryman (*The Unconquered Country*), Michael Swanwick (*The Iron Dragon's Daughter*), Gene Wolfe (*The Book of the New Sun*), Jane Yolen (*Briar Rose*) . . . and many other fine authors, too numerous to mention them all.

As a genre, it is a generous one, its readers open-minded, its practitioners good-natured enough to encourage the field's diversity, supporting a wide variety of books from the old pulp-style adventure tales to prismatic, fractured postmodern works . . . and everything in between. Like any limb on the Tree of Story, it has forked into many smaller branches: there's the branch of Humorous Fantasy; and Urban Fantasy with its punk-rock edge; and modern "swashbucklers" in which dialogue is as fast and sharp as a sword. There's contemporary Magic Realism, indistinguishable from that on the mainstream shelves. There are "Steampunks," a wild crew with their feet in the nineteenth century, their heads in cyberpunk technology (or maybe it's the other way around). There are "Mannerists" whose works hark back more to Austen and the Brontës than to Tolkien; while the tales of "gender-bending" writers twist like ivy around around several different branches. The puckish "pre-Joycean Fellowship" (whose name is a nod to the pre-Raphaelites) want to get back to old-fashioned storytelling values and well-structured plots; while The Young Trollopes, on the other hand, want to throw plot and structure out the window, concentrating on character instead. In short, the field of fantasy is much like the field of fiction as a whole: filled with both serious artists and hacks, with thoughtful theorists and just plain cranks, with writers on various soapboxes and writers just out to make a buck, or to go to the parties, or to change the world, or to write the Great American Novel.

One thing these fantasists do not do (unless they specifically choose to) is work in the kind of isolation our society generally attributes to writers. As artists in other literary "ghettos" have discovered, being marginalized from the broader mainstream tends to foster a sense of community. The fantasy community is a lively and gregarious one, meeting at writers' conventions held across England and America, interacting over computer networks and through the pages of critical magazines. As a result, a number of fantasy books are in dialogue with one another, their writers engaged in an ongoing discourse about the future of the field.

As you look through the following pages, you will also find a few unexpected faces: writers like Joyce Carol Oates and J. P. Donleavy, not generally thought of as fantasists. In fact, had we but time and room many more such writers could be included here, for fantasy—as a literary style—is not confined to the genre shelves. A number of writers from other disciplines have also walked through the magic lands that lie "beyond the fields we know" (to borrow a phrase from Lord Dunsany), infusing their work with magic, mythic, mystic, or ghostly elements—writers like Margaret Atwood (*Bluebeard's Egg*), Alice Hoffman (*Practical Magic*), Nancy Willard (*Sister Water*), Mark Helprin (*A Winter's Tale*), Toni Morrison (*Beloved*), Sara Maitland (*A Book of Spells*), Marina Warner (*Mermaids in the Basement*), Steven Millhauser (*Little Kingdoms*), Alasdair Gray (*Poor Things*), Salman Rushdie (*Haroun and the Sea of Stories*) and A. S. Byatt (*Possession*). In particular, the English writer Angela Carter has had a lasting impact on fantasy fiction with her brilliantly surrealistic novels and her dark adult fairy tales. (Her early death was a terrible loss to fantasy and mainstream readers alike.) Writers like Carter, Hoffman, Atwood, and Oates have been instrumental in opening mainstream literature to the possibilities inherent in the fantasy form.

At the same time, the magic realism to be found in the contemporary fiction of other lands (by writers like Nigeria's Ben Okri, Italy's Italo Calvino, Japan's Haruki Murakami, and most particularly the Latin American magic realists: Jorge Amado, Isabel Allende, Miguel Angel Asturias, the peerless Gabriel García Márquez, et al.) is influencing a new generation of writers all around the globe. This work has had a powerful effect within the fantasy genre; while in the mainstream, its influence is more evident with each passing year—particularly in quietly magical works by Chicano writers like Alfredo Vea Jr. (*La Maravilla*); Native American writers like Thomas King (*Green Grass Running Water*); and African American writers like Randall Kenan (*Let the Dead Bury Their Dead*) and Charlotte Watson Sherman (*Killing Color*). Books like these blur the strict lines drawn between mainstream and genre fiction, as do writers like Jonathan Carroll (*The Bones of the Moon*), Scott Bradfield (*Dream of the Wolf*), and Delia Sherman (*The Porcelain Dove*), with fiction published in both fields. Such cross-pollination serves to enrich all areas of literature, and I, for one, long for a day when these boundaries disappear.

I don't expect that day to come soon. At this point, strict genre lines are drawn not just by critics but by book marketers in order to facilitate easy stocking of bookstore shelves. Thus serious literary endeavors and light adventure novels for teenage boys will continue to sit side by side upon the fantasy shelves, often with identical dragons and swordsmen leering from the covers. What is the serious reader to do when confronted with such look-alike books? (Aside from investing in slipcase covers so you can read on the bus without embarrassment?) This is a field in which one must come equipped with reviews and recommendations in order to wade through the deluge of titles published every year. *The Year's Best Fantasy and Horror* anthology is an annual roundup of good short fiction, along with recommended reading lists for longer works to be found in both the mainstream and the genre; *Century* magazine is the field's first real literary journal; and *Locus* magazine provides thorough and intelligent reviews on a monthly basis.

You may have noticed that in these pages I have refrained from giving a hard-and-fast definition of "fantasy fiction," other than to toss around words like "mythic," "magical," "surrealist," "post-realist" . . . Better minds than mine have tried and failed to come up with a truly satisfying definition of a work of fantasy; it is, after all, the nature of faery (as J. R. R. Tolkien has reminded us) to be elusive and mutable. Those readers well versed in fantasy fiction know the feel, the look, the distinctive smell of a fantasy story when they come upon it; while for those new to the fantastic, let me send you to the source instead: to the wonderful stories, poems and novels that make up the fantasy field:

There are several excellent anthologies that provide an historical survey of the field: *Masterpieces of Fantasy and Enchantment* and *Masterpieces of Fantasy and Wonder* edited by David G. Hartwell; *The Fantastic Imagination, Vols. I and II* and *The Phoenix Tree* edited by Robert H. Boyer and Kenneth J. Zahorski; *The Oxford Book of Fantasy Stories* edited by Tom Shippey; *The Oxford Book of Modern Fairy Tales* edited by Alison Lurie; and *The Penguin Book of Modern Fantasy by Women* edited by A. Susan Williams and Richard Glyn Jones. Good nonfiction resources include: *Fantasists on Fantasy* edited by Boyer and Zahorski; *Classic Fantasy Writers* edited by Harold Bloom; *From the Beast to the Blonde: On Fairy Tales and Their Tellers* by Marina Warner, and "In the Tradition" by Michael Swanwick (reprinted in *The Year's Best Fantasy and Horror, Eighth Annual Collection*). For academic writings on the subject of fantasy literature, contact the International Association for the Fantastic in the Arts, Florida Atlantic University, College of Humanities, 500 NW 20th HU-50 BA, Boca Raton, FL 33431.

A proper history of fantasy fiction could fill the pages of this book, and I fear that this small attempt at it is inevitably inadequate. The books crowded on the shelves around me are already voicing their discontent: "What about C. L. Moore?" one cries. "What about Jonathan Swift?" says another. "What about Edward Eager, Mark Twain, P. L. Travers, Leonora Carrington? Jack Finney? Jack Vance? Poul Anderson? Avram Davidson? Evangeline Walton? What about all the dark fantasy writers like Edgar Allan Poe and Clark Ashton Smith?" Hush, I tell them, shaking my head. I simply can't write about them all. The tales they've given us speak more eloquently than I do, in any case.

The great mythologist Joseph Campbell once wrote, "Myth must be kept alive. The people who can keep it alive are the artists of one kind or another." Writers in the fantasy field are among the artists keeping myth alive. Those epic tales and fairy tales that speak to us from centuries long past have often taken the form of a quest: The hero is torn from hearth and home and set on a strange unpredictable road, where a trial must be endured, a riddle solved, a monster overcome, a future claimed. By the time of the quest's completion, something or someone has been transformed . . . most often the heroes themselves. Modern fantasy fiction also often takes the form of a quest: J. R. R. Tolkien's Frodo, Ursula K. Le Guin's Ged, John Crowley's Smokey and Auberon, Patricia A. McKillip's young Riddlemaster of Hed all undergo rites of initiation and transformation . . . and, in the process, effect the transformation of the worlds in which they live.

The fantasy quest is a dangerous one, as Ursula K. Le Guin warns us (in her essay "Dreams They Must Explain Themselves" from *The Language of the Night*). Fantasy, she says, is "not antirational, but pararational; not realistic, but surrealistic, a heightening of reality. In Freud's terminology, it employs primary, not secondary process thinking. It employs archetypes which, as Jung warned us, are dangerous things. Fantasy is nearer to poetry, to mysticism, and to insanity than naturalistic fiction is. It is a wilderness, and those who go there should not feel too safe. . . . A fantasy is a journey to the subconscious mind, just as psychoanalysis is. Like psychoanalysis, it can be dangerous, and *it will change you*."

This book, too, took the shape of a quest as photographer Patti Perret traveled across America, drove through English country lanes, and crossed over the Irish Sea in order to create the intimate portraits gathered within these pages. Like a fantasy tale, her journey was long and occasionally arduous, rewarded by moments of pure enchantment, captured by the camera lens.

Patti has been a photographer since receiving her first Brownie camera at a very young age. She went on to study in the fine arts department at Indiana University, where she admired the work of Robert Frank, Diane Arbus, Dorothea Lange, and Alfred Stiglitz. Patti has always been drawn to portraiture— even her photographs that are empty of people (clotheslines, backyards in Indiana, houses recently vacated) are nonetheless about people's lives. Moving to New York City, she photographed the street scenes of her colorful East Village neighborhood, and worked for the internationally known photojournalist Mary Ellen Mark. Through Mary Ellen Mark she had the opportunity to meet filmmaker Woody Allen, which resulted in a job with the production company of his film *Stardust Memories*. She then became the staff photographer for the television show *Saturday Night Live*, photographing the celebrity hosts in various locations around New York, and creating the montage of photographs that opened each show.

Through her musician husband, Mark Bingham, Patti met the musician Peter Stampfel and his wife, Betsy Wollheim, prominent in the science fiction publishing field. She thus became intrigued by tales of the "wild and wacky" science fiction community which seemed to stretch across the country like one big extended family. In the 1980s, eager to travel and to create a body of work on one subject, she spent a year on the road with Mark crisscrossing America, living out of the back of her car and taking the photographs that became *The Faces of Science Fiction*. In the twelve years since, she has relocated to her native city of New Orleans, where she continues to work in portraiture (with a particular interest in photographing dancers) and as a still photographer for feature films. Reading several magic realist books (particularly *Was*, by Geoff Ryman) set off Patti's desire to take photographs on the road once again—this time focused on the community of writers in the fantasy field. This time, with two young children to raise, she arranged a series of shorter trips, beginning the project in 1994, completing it in 1996.

Her journey began in Boston in an aura of magic: at Delia Sherman's turreted house, straight out of a fantasy tale with its gargoyled staircase, tall jeweled windows, and paintings of goblins and faeries. She arrived in time for a "Viennese" party hosted by Sherman and Ellen Kushner where guests arrived in period costume, waltzed, and performed a play. On the northeast coast, Lloyd Alexander and Susan Cooper are remembered for their graciousness; Nancy Springer for the peacefulness of the horse pasture where she rides each day; Lucius Shepard for kindly showing up despite being "sick as a dog" with the flu; Terry Goodkind for his house in the woods, built with his own hands. She encountered William Kotzwinkle on the same island where Goodkind lives. The writer was outdoors practicing tai chi, a large boom box beside him playing Kiri Te Kanawa (an Australian aboriginal artist) singing "I've Got You under My Skin" . . . a moment, said Patti, as surreal as those found in Kotzwinkle's books.

In Minneapolis, Patti was amazed by the tight-knit network of writers living there who work, play, argue, and make music together in various permutations. She received an enchanted tour of the green, wooded islands of the Pacific Northwest from Elizabeth Ann Scarborough; walked through the mist of Golden Gate Park in San Francisco with Katharine Kerr; and went to see Rodin's "Gates of Hell" with Tad Williams in Palo Alto. In Oklahoma, she was introduced to falconry by Misty Lackey; in South Carolina, she spent a night with Robert Jordan and his wife, Harriet McDougal, in their beautiful two-hundred-year-old house in historic Charleston.

In Ireland, she saw the Duffy Circus in Dublin ("a Fellini-esque experience"), had tea at J. P. Donleavy's manor, visited Katherine Kurtz at her castle, and was taken to an old Irish pub to hear music on the fourth of July. Diana Wynne Jones, on the Welsh-English border, allowed herself to be photographed despite recovering from a broken neck. Michael Scott Rohan arrived hot and weary in Oxford after hours on a broken-down train; Patti obligingly found a nice, cool medieval crypt in which to take his photograph. In Devon, she navigated the mazelike lanes to the village where I live, and gamely tramped through a wood thick with mud and briers, her cameras in tow. In London, Robert Holdstock was particularly charming, as were Garry Kilworth and his wife—and she met Geoff Ryman, whose heartrending book had started the whole journey off.

There were, naturally, many other people, towns, and adventures encountered along the way. The above are merely the few she recounts on the phone from her darkroom in New Orleans when I call—

catching her busy and distracted—on the day that she's finishing the prints. The journey ended, she tells me, with a car trip reminiscent of the travels for her previous book. Only this time, traveling through the Southwest, she was accompanied not only by her husband but by their two young children as well— meeting Lewis Shiner in Austin, Texas; eating a late dinner with L. Sprague de Camp; traveling on to Arizona to see Judith Tarr and her horses. The last stop was New Mexico, in a country town between Albuquerque and Santa Fe, where Patti photographed George R. R. Martin at a party on New Year's Eve. She had photographed George twelve years before, for *The Faces of Science Fiction*. "He hadn't changed. It was as if he wore the exact same glasses, the same jacket, the same hat. My books had come full circle for me, and that's when the journey was complete."

Each portrait in this book, Patti says, is the result of a collaboration between writer and photographer. "The relationships I've had with these writers have been brief, and yet also intense. One needs to go beyond the surface, beyond the setting, to a place of trust—achieving a level of intimacy, a kind of non-verbal communication that allows the magic to happen and to be captured by the camera. This, I've discovered—as I've traveled and talked to so many writers of fantasy—is the similarity between our two fields. We're all trying to capture magic."

The Faces of Fantasy

Kristine Kathryn Rusch

FOR YEARS I HAVE PONDERED the "whys" of fiction. Why do human beings need story? Why do we enjoy story? Why do we think story is important?

I have no scientific answer.

I have an unscientific one, based on gut and personal experience. Fiction is communication, a way of seeing intimately into another life, a way of living that other life. We are isolated creatures. Fiction diminishes that isolation.

Fiction also provides hope where there is none, adventure where none exists, and dreams where none are possible.

Fiction is central to who we are. In my opinion, it is what makes us human.

Author of *Traitors, The White Mists of Power, The Sacrifice . . .*

Lloyd Alexander

AFTER NEARLY A DOZEN YEARS of writing realism for adults, I felt an indefinable, irresistible urge to write a fantasy for young people. Not for any specific child; but, rather, because I believed it could be a powerful and serious literary form. It turned out to be the most creative and liberating experience of my life, letting me draw on my own deepest feelings far more than I had ever done.

Since then, my books have been children's fantasies—a term I don't find very expressive or descriptive. In the same way that I see no essential difference in writing for adults or young people, I see no conflict between realism and fantasy. Both try to illuminate human relationships, conflicts, and moral dilemmas. I do admit that I much prefer fantasy. To me, it has the emotional strength of a dream, it works directly on our nerve endings, whatever age we happen to be, touching heights and depths not always accessible through realism. In fantasy, my concern is how we learn to be real human beings. It's a continuing process.

Author of *The Black Cauldron, The Book of Three, Taran Wanderer* . . .

Joyce Carol Oates

TO BE ENTRANCED, to be driven, to be obsessed, to be under the spell of an emerging, not quite yet fully "comprehended" narrative—this is the great happiness of the writer's life, even as it burns us out and exhausts us, unfitting us for the placid contours of "normality."

Author of Zombie, Heat and Other Stories, The Poisoned Kiss . . .

J. P. Donleavy

HAVING BEEN A PAINTER before becoming an author taught me that the written word traveled farther and reached deeper and into more minds than a painting, and was also something, once published, no amount of tearing up or a boot through the canvas could destroy or stop. Also there is the satisfaction that the written word could willy-nilly penetrate and annoy people in the privacy of their own homes. And the greater justice could be done as their immediate resentments might anger them enough to put dents in their more valuable pieces of antique furniture. Or words might instead touch their sensibilities so that they know they listen to a kindred soul.

Author of *The Ginger Man, The Beastly Beatitudes of Balthazar B,*
The Destiny of Darcy Dancer, Gentleman . . .

Alan Garner

THE JOB OF A STORYTELLER is to speak the truth. But what we feel most deeply can't be spoken in words alone. At this level, only images connect. And here, story becomes symbol; symbol is myth. And myth is truth.

So I live, at all times, for imaginative fiction; for ambivalence, not for instruction. When language serves dogma, story is lost. I live also, and only, for excellence. My care is not for the cult of egalitarian mediocrity that has swept the world, wherein even the critics are no longer qualified to differentiate, but for literature, which I would define as words that provoke response.

I am not alone in my concern that commodity, not quality, is in demand now: the immaculate rubbish that we produce so well. Consciousness is on the move. Something is at work: a recognition of crisis, of the banal and the shoddy in human affairs. Recently an Australian Aboriginal shaman warned me, "The serpent has woken. Jarapiri stirs. The earth shakes. And the warriors are gathering."

Author of The Weirdstone of Brisingamen, The Owl Service, The Lad of the Gad . . .

M. John Harrison

"What we need here is a dream, he told himself,
a little something to get by on."

—Robert Stone, *Children of Light*

Author of *The Committed Men*, the Viriconium sequence, *Climbers* . . .

Terri Windling

I WAS TOLD AT AN IMPRESSIONABLE AGE that "writers should write about what they know." I wanted to write magical fiction, so I have endeavored to lead a magical life. Living comes first, and stories come after—to shape life, explore it, embellish it, explain it, to praise and damn and understand it; to "celebrate without cease," (as Barbara Kingsolver has written) "the good luck of getting set down here on a lively earth." Fairy tales, like myths and poetry, use a language that cuts to the heart of truth. I write about art, paint pictures about stories, and live as truthfully as I can.

When Patti came to my English village, the dust of Ireland on her heels and cameras slung around her neck, I took her to a ruined tower hidden in a wood nearby. There is an old fairy tale about a brother and sister who live at the heart of such a wood. The brother, stumbling upon enchantment, is trapped each day in the shape of a deer. He returns to his sister's side at dusk, shaped as a man when the sun goes down, but at dawn he must wrap himself in the white deerskin and transform once more. While he sleeps, the sister brushes the dirt and leaves and thorns from the white deerskin, tending the tattered hide with care so no harm will come to him. Yet of course, harm comes. A king travels to the wood to bring down the magnificent deer. Although it is a man he hunts, it is the woman he will catch, wounding her soft heart with love as his arrows wound her brother's flesh. These are the choices the story offers to this steadfast, silent girl: She can love her brother, take care of him, and send the king and his arrows away; she can love the king and be taken care of, locked away in his castle.

And yet there is another choice the old tale doesn't speak of. I see her clearly: standing in the doorway while her brother sleeps. She is running her hand down the silken hide, smelling its scent of musk and moss, imagining muscles bunched beneath, dreaming of motion, freedom, and flight. Her brother sleeps. The king awaits. The forest is dark, wild, unknown; a river sings beyond the oaks and the red rowan berries are glowing like jewels. She picks up the skin, and wraps it around her slim shoulders. The sun is rising.

Author of The Wood Wife, The Green Children, editor of The Armless Maiden . . .

Anne McCaffrey

I TURNED SEVENTY YEARS OLD on the first of April, 1996, an age I really never expected to reach even if I don't think of myself as "aged" . . . until I start to get out of a chair and realize that the joints don't respond as freely as they once did. I gave myself the party . . . taking over a restaurant that has been one of my favorite eating places for the past fifteen years: The Tree of Idleness in Bray, County Wicklow. I celebrated with good friends and relatives.

I've lived in Ireland now over a quarter of a century and never regretted the move. I live in a house I designed with mod cons that include a heated indoor swimming pool and bookshelves everywhere, built on the forty-seven acres of land I farm, with splendid views of horses gamboling in the field beyond my garden and green Irish hills. I don't mind the rain: I can always write a sunny scene if the weather bothers me, which it rarely does.

My children are moving back to Ireland, too: Georgeanne married a charming Irishman; Alec, Kate, and their two children, Eliza and Amelia, arrived from New Jersey just before Christmas, and we're working hard on Todd, Jenna, and Ceara Rose to leave Los Angeles.

When I was growing up, my mother used to say, "Anne, you're going to go to college, get married, and have children. But what do you intend to do with the rest of your life?" Not a question most parents were asking girl children in the 1930s. Not even the wildest guess would have been accurate or as fantastic as how I am spending the "rest of my life."

I never knew SF existed until 1950! Bless Edmond Hamilton for *The Star Kings* yarn that first hooked me. Bless Andre Norton for *Daybreak 2000* and James Blish's *Cities in Flight* and Robert Silverberg and Gordon Dickson who also helped me immerse myself in this *genre*. And especially bless Virginia Kidd, my estimable agent, whose invaluable criticism guided me firmly to the *New York Times* best-seller list.

Coincidentally, this year marks the thirtieth year of the existence of Pern, for I began to write the short story to improve the press of dragons in the spring of 1966. If "To boldly go" did well for *Star Trek*, "Lessa Woke, Cold" did a great deal for me. Both series have enjoyed a certain robust, and totally unexpected, longevity.

As I said, I'm seventy this year but, if I am slower than I was at fifty, I'm scarcely retired. Other professions get to retire: writers don't. There's always that book I wanted to write and haven't got around to yet. Another story pops into my head serendipitously and then I'm away again on a new adventure.

Author of *The White Dragon, Dragonriders of Pern, Dragonsinger . . .*

Peter Straub

HERE IS A DEEP WOOD, HERE IS A PATH. Gene Ammons was playing "I'm Afraid the Masquerade Is Over" or "I'm Beginning to See the Light" or "Song of the Islands," I'm not sure, with Walter Bishop Jr. or Patti Brown on piano, Arthur Davis or George Duvivier on bass, Art Taylor on drums, and Ray Baretto on congas. For them, it is mid-October 1961, in Englewood Cliffs, New Jersey. My son Ben, seventeen on this ravishing Sunday in the middle of November 1994, leaned through the door and said, "I came here to laugh." I'm a face of fantasy, he ought to laugh. Patti Perret asked, "Who are we listening to?" "Gene Ammons," I said. "He's really good." Nothing like understatement. I was wondering what a particular old boy was about to say to a particular woman, both of these people being vibrantly present and alive in spite of what may seem the handicap of also being fictional. For them it is the evening of a humid Tuesday in mid-August 1993, in Amherst, Massachusetts, and over whatever the old boy, on the whole a sympathetic fellow despite his manner, is about to say hovers the remark of another character, an elderly lady excluded from this conversation, that muses and angels disturb the air, raise great gusts of wind. We are still in the wood, but a hundred yards back, the path disappeared. It is night, what else, it is always night, and there are no maps. I don't mind, leave this part to me, if there's one thing I'm used to it is the utter absence of maps. A little while later in another room, my daughter, fourteen in November of 1994, wandered into the frame and speculated about the fantasies of those who might see her photographed with me in a book. My daughter makes her own maps, I guess. I came here to laugh. Gene Ammons, boy, when he had his horn in his mouth that guy couldn't make a mistake.

Author of Shadowland, Ghost Story, The Throat . . .

Poppy Z. Brite

(Journal entry, 16 October 1988)

STILL I NEED TO GET BACK into journal writing—how have I become so damned conscious of technique? A result of swollen ego, that's what. I got to believing at the tender age of 21 that I was already well on my way to becoming a Master of Technique. (1) I have a long way to go yet and (2) do I *want* to be a Master of Technique? Is that a title I wish to have bestowed upon me? What about the magic? The absolute goddamn magic of writing. The way I sat at the typewriter and wrote "Missing" and "The Georgia Story," and I don't remember writing either of them except for the very beginnings, because after that I slipped into magic. Fell through the hole in the paper. Was I thinking about "technique" then? Was I thinking "Hmm, this is a clever word choice, I wonder if the reader will appreciate it."

But I must not censure myself too much; it is a rewriting mentality. I've never had to rewrite a novel before, never had to stay in that mentality for so long. You are supposed to go through the manuscript judging, changing, tightening. Or Monica's recipe: "A little more purple there, a little less purple here, a red sunset there, a whiskey stain over there."

Note: This journal trails off in midword halfway through. Except for travel diaries, it was the last one I ever kept.

PZB, 10 March 1996

Author of Lost Souls, Drawing Blood, Wormwood...

P. C. Hodgell

WHEN I WAS A CHILD GROWING UP in my grandmother's house, I had a recurrent dream that there were three of me living in a land beyond the sunset. More than that I can't remember, except for the image of three children with my face, crowded into the front seat of a tiny, shiny car going . . . somewhere.

I grew up. I became three different people.

"Pat" is the closest to that child of long ago, still living in the old, family home, still shy and solitary, with the relics of her childhood crusted about her like layers of pearl around a grain of sand. She thinks it very strange to find herself in the pages of such a book as this and wonders (but doesn't ask) if there may not have been some mistake.

"Patricia C.," on the other hand, is impatient to get on with lesson plans. This fall she will teach a college course based on books that she hasn't read since graduate school. *Beowulf.* *The Faerie Queene. Paradise Lost.* She touches her doctorate as if it were a talisman. She has earned this. It means something.

"What?" asks Pat.

"Shut up," says Patricia C.

"P. C." pays no attention to either of them. What does their bickering matter when her heroine Jame is about to ride into the military college of Tentir and fall off her horse at the feet of the Commandant? This will only be the first act in a year's worth of misadventures, culminating (somehow) in Jame's graduation as a cadet officer. She will earn it. It will mean something.

"What?" asks Pat. "Will it make me enough money to go on living in my old house forever and ever?"

"What?" demands Patricia C. "Will a fantasy, a mere genre work, earn me any respect in academia?"

Jammed between them in the front seat of a Honda Civic, P. C. doesn't answer, hasn't heard. While Patricia C. stares grimly ahead at four long, bleak months of classes and Pat gazes uneasily out the side window at a present sliding inexorably into the past, P. C. happily draws a map of a land that never was, beyond the sunset.

Where are these three middle-aged women going?

Ask P. C. She has the map.

Author of *Godstalk, Dark of the Moon, Seeker's Mask* . . .

Tad Williams

"WHERE DO YOU GET YOUR IDEAS?"

Most writers hate that frequently asked question, but I regard it as a not-too-onerous tax for having an imagination.

See, most people know that ideas are free and words are cheap, so they figure there has to be *something* different about writers (otherwise everyone would be doing it). And they're right (although they seem a little disappointed when we try to explain where our ideas actually come from, which has nothing to do with mysterious catalogue companies or alien radio transmissions). We also need to point out that there's more to this writing thing than just inspiration—it's work, too. Seeds and dirt are as readily available as words, but that doesn't mean anyone can be a farmer, a gardener, or a landscaper.

Actually, for me, *writing* is not the point, *making things* is the point. If I construct something that has its own peculiar truth or beauty, and can then share it with others, I'm a happy guy. I'm not one of those writers who couldn't have been anything else. I would have been very cheerful directing films, or disturbing public places with huge murals, or spending weeks in a studio writing and producing music.

Writing is nice, though. It's a very quiet indulgence. Working on a novel appeases my tyrannical, control-freak side in a way that making a film never would. For one thing, I get to do *everything*—scripting, set design, casting, makeup, costumes, editing—and I can usually convince the actors to do what I want them to. Usually.

Also, I get to stay up late, sleep in, lie around and stare at the ceiling, and people have to take my word that I'm working. Joy!

The longer you write, the more you become aware of your own inner voices speaking through your work. I've learned a lot about myself by paying attention to my own repeating themes. In fact, I think of my works of fiction as yearbook entries from the School of My Life.

I hope I get to do quite a few more before I graduate.

Author of Tailchaser's Song, To Green Angel Tower, The Dragonbone Chair . . .

Storm Constantine

I BEGAN WRITING IN CHILDHOOD by creating stories I'd always wanted to read. Fantasy attracted me as a genre because its limitless boundaries allowed me to indulge my wildest imaginings. I never sent any of my work off to publishers until, in my mid-twenties, a dread of reaching thirty and being stuck in a regular job gave me the courage to start taking my writing more seriously. I was lucky enough to be accepted by the first publisher I sent a manuscript to, and have since escaped from the day job so that I can write full-time.

I'm inspired by dreams and shadows, obsessions and desire. By nature, I'm a dream collector and never stop working. I question people about their weirdest dreams and the strangest, most inexplicable experiences they've had. All this information whirls around in my mind, and new dreams emerge that form the seeds of stories and novels.

Author of the Wraeththu trilogy, *The Monstrous Regiment, Burying the Shadow* . . .

Margaret Weis

WRITING FANTASY provides me the opportunity to discuss and comment on issues and concerns facing people today. My goal is to lure my readers into thinking about and reflecting upon serious subjects such as racism, religious intolerance, alcoholism, and warfare even as they fondly imagine they are using the books to escape the "real world."

Author of the Dragonlance Chronicles, the Darksword trilogy (both with Tracy Hickman), *Rose of the Prophet* . . .

Delia Sherman

I LOVE COSTUMES AND MASKS because they are magic rings that work in the real world. They alter the face you show to the world, protect you from prying eyes, manipulate perceptions. The proper clothes and the proper attitude can transform a quiet, middle-aged fantasy writer into a great lady, an adventurer, a waif, a scholar, a lady's maid, even a man, if you don't look too closely. But they can't show anything that's not already present underneath. If you want to reveal your soul beyond all possibility of denial, wear a mask. Or write fantasy. It's essentially the same thing.

Author of *Through a Brazen Mirror, The Porcelain Dove,* "The Printer's Daughter" . . .

Michael Scott Rohan

WHY DO I WRITE FANTASY? For the same reason I write anything—because I enjoy reading it, and the sources from which it springs. As a small child I devoured (not literally!) the *Larousse Mythology,* with its vivid illustrations. I still do. Discovering authors like Tolkien, Leiber, Avram Davidson, Bulgakov, and others was like slotting new pieces into a puzzle. The idea of passing on some of what I've received, becoming part of the same process, is incredibly satisfying. I believe strongly that we need the ancient archetypes that linger on behind our language and our thought, and that in re-creating them we revitalize ourselves. Today, perhaps only science has something of the same aura—hence science fiction, which I also write. Music, though, taps deeper wells, and it's both my other professional interest and fuel for my imagination. Everything from folk rock to Rimsky-Korsakov, Mozart, Monteverdi, film music to Sibelius and Wagner flows through it.

For me, though, what sparks off fantasy most strongly is hard reality. Magical swords are forged with real metal and real sweat, and you sail off into the sunset on a real windjammer—real wood, real canvas, and most of all, a real crew.

I've little patience with people who carp about escapism. Escape is a natural, healthy instinct, and central to all literature. Every writer, even the most hidebound social realist, creates his own subjective world, operating according to his laws and peopled with creatures that dance to his tune. The anti-escapist only wants to narrow our choices. Ask yourself, as Tolkien suggested to C. S. Lewis, who is most interested in preventing escape.

Gaolers.

Author of Cloud Castles, The Gates of Noon, Chase the Morning . . .

Lewis Shiner

I SPENT A LOT OF TIME AND ENERGY early on fighting labels. Lately I find I don't really object to being called a fantasy writer. I think there is a fantasy element in virtually everything I've ever written—not in the high-fantasy sense of magic or dragons, but in the more intimate, psychological sense. That knife-edge where people's dreams and desires intersect reality seems to call me back again and again.

Author of Glimpses, Deserted Cities of the Heart, Slam . . .

Patricia Kennealy-Morrison

MY STORIES COME TO ME via a portal located six inches above the typewriter and a foot beyond it. I just reach through and pull them onto the page, usually kicking and screaming. (The stories, not me.) (Well, sometimes me.)

I am, in that sense, the first reader of my own novels. Very often they surprise me. I have less to say than you might think in how the tales tell themselves; I'm just the typist. The books are a gift, right enough; but they are not *my* gift. Rather, they are given *to* me; this makes me feel quite humble, and also very, very proud.

Kennealy means Wolf's Head in Irish. The name is said to denote a clan of hereditary Celtic tribal shamans: folk whose job it is to journey to another creation and fetch home truth and vision for the people. I have followed in the family business, as it were, as witch and priestess, since I was seventeen years old; as a writer, since the day I learned to print.

When you write fiction, the trick is to learn when or where or whether life is imitating art or art is imitating life. When you write fantasy, the task is to find the line between what's real and what is more real than the real. And fantasy is the instrument given us by the Creator of Being to enable us to distinguish truth from mere fact. As fantasists (or shamans), we are called to weave upon a loom unlike all others', a weft that is built to last.

On Midsummer Day 1970 I wedded, in a Celtic ceremony more magical than any fantasy any of us in this book ever created, a man best known for singing "Light My Fire," though all my beautiful Jim ever really wanted to be known for was, like any good fantasist, any good shaman, his own fetching home of truth and vision for the people. Some of those people, these days, actually worship him as a god. (Not all fantasies, alas, are to do with the truth; or even with the facts.) I say that this makes me a goddess by marriage, but my editor says not.

We'll see.

Author of The Copper Crown, The Throne of Scone, The Silver Branch . . .

R. A. Salvatore

I WAS AT A CONVENTION IN SEATTLE, giving a seminar about publishing, when a young man accused my writing of being cliché. "Why do the good guys always win?" he wanted to know.

Cliché? I don't think so. It's not a cliché that good overcomes evil; it's a philosophy. In my books, good will almost always overcome evil (but not without great cost sometimes), because I believe that good is stronger than evil. We have developed a distorted view of what makes a hero. Too often in the movies, or in other entertainment media, the hero is determined by who carries the biggest gun, or by who is borderline crazy enough to walk into seemingly impossible situations. Whatever happened to virtue and truth, and a belief in something larger and greater than ourselves?

These are the basis for spirituality, and also, I would argue, the basis for heroism. And these elements, by simple definition, are usually lacking on the side of evil. So yes, I answer to that guy in Seattle. Good wins. Because that's the way it's supposed to be.

Author of Dragonslayer, The Sword of Bedwyr, Night Masks . . .

Raymond E. Feist

FANTASY? I don't know exactly what that is. By the broadest definition of the term, all fiction is fantasy. What I write are adventure novels, with a magic element. I try to look at my work as historical novels of a place that doesn't exist, and view my characters as recognizable contemporary characters who happen to live in an amazing and improbable place. Those who seek some deep significance in the work are welcome to do so, but no matter what they tell you in General Literature 101, there isn't always a hidden agenda, some character doesn't always represent the author's point of view, and there isn't always a deeper message. My only intent is to entertain. If you found something deeper than amusement in the work, count it a bonus. If you just had fun, I did my job.

Author of *Magician, The King's Buccaneer, Shadow of a Dark Queen* . . .

Diana Wynne Jones

MY FAMILY FINDS ME A NUISANCE when I'm writing a book. It isn't just that I get absentminded and forget meals. I laugh. In the early days, when I was writing *The Ogre Downstairs,* I sat by myself and laughed so much that my children kept coming and asking if I was all right. Later, they got used to it and simply tested me to make sure I'd heard what they said. I became very good at replaying a conversation I hadn't actually known I'd had. Now, when the children have long ago grown up, my husband still gets astonished when I laugh as I write. When I was writing *Howl's Moving Castle* and nearly fell off the sofa in my mirth, he said, "You *can't* be making *yourself* laugh!" I said, "No, it's this book that's making me laugh." That is because, when a book is going as it should, it doesn't feel as if I'm doing it. It takes its own way, and people in it do things I don't expect. This is true however a book comes to me. *Charmed Life* arrived in my head almost as a complete book, but it was still unexpected. With *Archer's Goon,* on the other hand, I had almost no idea what was going to happen from one page to the next—which made it *very* unexpected.

But I don't always laugh. Some books, like the Dalemark quartet, have kept me on the edge of my seat, barely able to breathe. Others, like *Fire and Hemlock* and *Dogsbody,* have wrung my heart as I wrote them and taught me things I never thought I knew about people and their feelings.

I *learn* things as I write, you see. This is why I enjoy it so much. And I want to know what happens next. If I don't want to know, I stop. And I want other people to have the same experience from a book that I had when I was writing it. Reading a book should be an *experience* in every meaning of the word, but it should be an experience people enjoy. To my great pleasure, people do seem to enjoy my books—and not children only. Some years back I was stunned to discover that large numbers of adults read and enjoy them alongside fantasy specially written for adults. I think this may be because the books always arrange themselves around timeless stories as I write them. Nearly every one of my books has pulled in myths, folktales, or legends as it went along, and these things can have something to say to everyone.

Author of *Dogsbody, Charmed Life, Fire and Hemlock . . .*

William Kotzwinkle

ALL OF LIFE is a fantasy.

Ursula K. Le Guin

FANTASY IS THE OLDEST KIND OF FICTION, and though it's forever finding new forms, it doesn't change in essence. So I don't really have anything new to add to what I said about fantasy in a couple of essays I wrote in 1974 (which can be found in my book *The Language of the Night*). Even through the flood of trite trilogies and formula fantasoids of the last twenty years, the real stuff keeps on being written, published, and read. Not even capitalism can kill the imagination.

In "Why Are Americans Afraid of Dragons?" I said, "Fantasy is true, of course. It isn't factual, but it is true. Children know that. Adults know it too, and that is precisely why many of them are afraid of fantasy. They know that its truth challenges, even threatens, all that is false, all that is phony, unnecessary, and trivial in the life they have let themselves be forced into living. They are afraid of dragons, because they are afraid of freedom."

And at the end of "The Child and the Shadow": "Fantasy is the language of the inner self. I will claim no more for fantasy than to say I personally find it the appropriate language in which to tell stories to children—and others. But I say that with some confidence, having behind me the authority of a very great poet, who put it much more boldly. 'The great instrument of moral good,' Shelley said, 'is imagination.' "

Author of *A Wizard of Earthsea, The Tombs of Atuan, Tehanu . . .*

Joel Rosenberg

FIRST SLIDE, PLEASE. Me as a baby. Nineteen fifty-four—RCA had just introduced color television. It was the year of *Brown v. Board of Education,* the first successful kidney transplant and Elvis's first commercial record. Ray Kroc started McDonald's; France begged for the United States to bail them out at Dien Bien Phu. Einstein was still alive, but he wasn't going to be much longer. We lived in North Dakota, then moved to Connecticut. I'd discuss my remarkably dysfunctional family-of-origin, but I said I'd keep this short, so: Two-thirds of abused kids don't go on to be abusers; I'm part of that majority.

Next slide. January 1979: me screaming in pain and clutching my right foot. That was the year of Thor Power Tool. The Shah fled Iran and left it to the Ayatollah; Jerry Falwell founded the Moral Majority. John Wayne died of cancer. It was the year of Three Mile Island, Donna Summers's Bad Girls, and the Sony Walkman. I was working at a home for the mentally retarded. One of the folks I was taking care of slammed the door on my toe—hard. Right then, I realized that if I was a science fiction and fantasy writer, this wouldn't be happening.

Next slide. Halloween, 1981: me bent over the keyboard of an electric typewriter. Walter Cronkite had retired; Charles and Diana were recently married. MTV launched itself; IBM released the original PC. Felicia and I were living in Willimantic, Connecticut, in a one-bedroom apartment. I was a bookkeeper; Felicia was waitressing. I stayed up all night writing the first chapters of my first novel.

Next slide, now: me in front of a computer screen, a brace on my right wrist to minimize carpal tunnel syndrome. The office is a mess; every time I think about cleaning it, I get back to work. O. J. Simpson was declared not guilty of his two murders, and thousands cheered in the streets; Bosnians are begging the United States to protect them from Serbian "ethnic cleansing." Yassir Arafat lives on the West Bank; Newt Gingrich is Speaker of the House; Sonny Bono's a congressman.

Last slide: me and the family. I live in what was a duplex in south Minneapolis, with my wife of seventeen years, our two daughters, my baby sister (who's now twenty-five), five cats, one dog, a couple dozen fish, and two computers. Writing is the softest touch I've ever had and the hardest dollar I've ever earned; I get up every morning, take the dog for a brisk walk, shower, and head downstairs to the office. Every weekday at 4:12 I go to the door to see the school bus drop off Judy, my five-year-old, then she and I head out to pick up her baby sister, Rachel, from daycare, and I spend the next hours, until the girls are in bed, being a daddy.

And I like all of that a lot.

Author of *D'Shai, The Warrior Lives, The Sleeping Dragon . . .*

Louise Cooper

THOUGH I WRITE FOR A LIVING, to me it isn't work. It's a way to explore and extend and celebrate my existence; to create and, for a while, live in worlds that simply can't be found in the here and now, and that call to my imagination and sense of adventure . . . and that yearning *something* that I can't define but which, perhaps, we all have inside us. Whether I'm writing for adults or for children, I want above all to tell a story. My whole purpose, as I see it, is to *entertain,* and if I ever forget that principle, then it'll be time to give my word processor a decent burial. I don't think that will happen, though. Even if I live to the age of one hundred I'll never stop imagining, or dreaming . . . or writing. And that's just the way I want it to be.

Author of the Time Master trilogy, *Sleep of Stone, Revenant* . . .

Marion Zimmer Bradley

I HAVE BEEN WRITING, quite literally, ever since I could hold a pen. My mother used to say I was lazy, because I never wanted to do anything but sit around and write or read. I think that's why I became an editor; now there's nothing I *have* to do but sit around and read and write and read. The quality of what I read in the slush pile isn't always as high as it might be, but I keep hoping. . . .

Fantasy was my first love, from the day I learned to read. It deals in the inner truth, the hopes and fears common to all humanity. It forces us to confront our archetypes, the core of our own spirits, our hearts and our minds. What we discover when we read or write fantasy is our eternal truth, free from the "where" and "when" of daily life, transformed into something more real than "real life."

Author of *The Mists of Avalon*, *The Forest House*, the Darkover series . . .

Michael Moorcock

I'M OFTEN ASKED BY BEGINNING AUTHORS for advice on writing fantasy fiction. I always say the same thing first—stop reading fantasy. Read literary fiction, other genres, nonfiction—anything but fantasy. One of the great problems with a form that turns into a commercial genre is that the genre traits themselves begin to dominate the work. Publishers even begin to select authors by the degree to which they replicate those traits. You start to develop a folk art.

Much of today's commercial fantasy seems to me to have similar qualities to degenerated Xeroxes, largely, I suspect, because the authors have read very little else but their favorite genre. This may be very cozy for them, but it is deadly for the fiction. Most of the authors who helped create today's existing genres were not writing in anything like an orthodox or established tradition—they drew their inspiration from many, many different sources, and it was this that gave their work its originality and vitality.

This is perhaps why I am so antipathetic to retail categories in fiction. I look forward to the day when I can again walk into any bookshop and see only a fiction category, arranged alphabetically so that you can find Jonathan Carroll where you look for Angela Carter, Raymond Carver, or Catullus, or William Shatner sharing a shelf with William Shakespeare. Nobody need be afraid that I, or any other reader, will confuse one with the other—but sometimes taking down either could introduce me to something engrossing, stimulating, and entertaining that I might otherwise never have discovered. In literature, as in society, the more we are divided, the more easily we are controlled. . . .

Author of The Eternal Champion; The Silver Warriors; Gloriana, or the Unfulfill'd Queen: Being a Romance . . .

Evangeline Walton

FOR ME IT STARTED SIXTY YEARS AGO when I wrote *The Virgin and the Swine* (since retitled *The Island of the Mighty*). But the stories were alive long before. Since I was a child, the old stories were told to me; and long, long ago, before I or my parents were born, millennia before.

There were always tales passed from mother to daughter, from father to son. Down through generations they came, so that we would never forget that place, that magic, that elemental and awesome power that abided in our forbears. In each generation the power of the tales rests with us, the storytellers. I weep, I cry with joy, I exult in the God-power of the words.

And so I have tried to pass them to another generation, to keep alive the mortal power of our earlier selves, even as the world changes and dies, sleeps and wakes anew to the force that gives life to our souls. So that some child can hear the tales and find them awakened in herself to pass to yet another generation. It is an unending joy and charge . . . opening to us an endless renewal of the force that beckons to us, as it did in times past to Don, Math, Gwydion, the old gods— the creative power that births the world anew with each new life.

Author of Witch House, Prince of Annwn, The Island of the Mighty . . .

John Crowley

EXCEPT AS CATEGORIES useful to publishers and booksellers, there is probably no such thing as "fantasy writing" and no "fantasy novels" that one could, or ought to, aspire to write. There are romances of many kinds, some of which contain quests, or magical helpers, or impossible coincidences, or realms not on the maps we consult in our nonreading lives; some do not. Certain such romances are today labeled "fantasy" by marketers of books, some are not. Some are called "novels" or "stories." Some are written by me. I would like as many people as possible to at least take up the ones I have written and look into them; I would like as many of those people as possible to then read and be touched by them. If such readers are deliberately in search of stories they call "fantasies," I would like them to regard my books, at least at first, as fantasies. If they have or think they have no interest in books so labeled, then I hope they never guess mine might be called so.

Author of *Ægypt; Little, Big; The Great Work of Time . . .*

Greer Ilene Gilman

SHE UNDOES

She undoes her hair,
    unbraiding to the wind
        the bright—it's thin now,
    falling to the comb, November,
cold in coming—bright as leaves
        her hair.
The bone pins bristle;
       she is wrists
and elbows.
      Knees.
Shy as dryad (virginal),
    the old girl's wild,
      the dark
         and cloudrush
           of the sky
her mind, her nightlong riding
         boneward.
      Bloodrags sail.
        (The moon
Wanes)
      "Done."
        "Undone."
          "And all to do,"
her sisters cry.
      Her selves. Unselving
        in the dark, the midwood.

Ah, they all go bare
    and they live by the air,
       sings Mally.
In and out her hands, the long swift
    stiffened hands unbraiding
        bear the stars, the seven
          Pleiades her ring.
      Orion is her comb.
The braid's undone.
      She shakes it, falling
        lightloose bright about her,
to her knees, as long
    as to her feet. She stands
      knee deep in dreams.
Unspelled, they scatter.
     A
        and
          O,
      they whirl away.
       No more.
No matter.
Let them rake her,
    cries Sibyl with her hands.
And nightlong
    winterlong her owl-
        winged hair's
          unbound.
She will not do it up.

Author of *Moonwise*

Elizabeth Ann Scarborough

GROWING UP IN A TIME WHEN THE EARTH, at least, has largely been not only explored, but most of the mysterious places paved and developed, logged or mined, industrialized or leveled by war or fire, I've always felt a great thirst for mysteries. Fantasy and science fiction, more than any other types of fiction, allow me to explore those mysteries, ancient, modern, and yet to be discovered or defined. When I was young I grieved that unless I became an astronaut I would never have anything to explore on this earth, but lately, as I look at the world with the eyes and mind of a fantasy writer, I discover that the modern world with its constant shifts and changes is a perpetual mystery machine. No matter what the technology or the destruction or the shifts in society, human nature is much the same, and I think it is the effects of change of one sort or another on people (and animals) that makes a good yarn. The sameness provides the mythic resonance and comforting familiarity and the changes themselves the new territory to be explored. The collision of the familiar and the new bring the characters, and sometimes the writer and reader as well, into both internal and external discoveries that can happily provide that much-touted "sense of wonder."

Author of *The Godmother, The Healer's War, Nothing Sacred* . . .

Charles de Lint

MYTHS AND FOLKTALES FASCINATE ME—not only for their story content and how they resonate against who I am, but for how they came to be in the first place. Though my stories usually explore a juxtaposing of old mythic matter with the modern world, or enthusiastically embrace what Jan Harold Brunvand calls "Urban Legends"—contemporary folktales and myths—occasionally I'll dabble in the origins of myths as well, wandering back into some never-was secondary world to visit an island or two in my own little archipelago, off in some distant corner of Jung's sea of shared consciousness.

Neither type of story is more important than the other. What is important is that they are as true as I can tell them; true not so much in a literal sense as in one that allows the passage of truths between my readers and myself. Or as Jane Yolen so eloquently has put it, a sentiment that I quote whenever I can: "Touch magic, pass it on."

Whether dealing with present-day concerns such as child abuse or homelessness, or the more timeless considerations of mythic matter and its inherent mysteries, the one thing I hope my writing does beyond its entertainment value is help the dialogue to continue.

Author of *Svaha, Memory and Dream, Moonheart . . .*

Lucius Shepard

WRITING IS A PRIVATE ACT WITH A PUBLIC RESULT, and the processes of that private act are generally haphazard, illogical, and trivial, a petty kind of magic whose intricacies one can no more remember than one can describe the pattern of one's thoughts as they emerge from wherever thoughts are kept. Thus it seems to me that to talk about my work and affect any sort of expertise concerning it would be sheer pretense. The words I've written are in all their flaws and virtues mysterious to me. Unfamiliar. I cannot recall thinking the thoughts that inspired them, and I have even less an idea of the person who wrote them. As a result, I feel far more comfortable talking about what I intend rather than what I've done. And yet I feel limited even in that regard. Obviously I have in my heart, as do most people, a desire to do more than I have done and somehow to increase the earth, but when I try to set down what exactly I intend, I usually end up making statements that are frivolous, pompous, silly, or simplistic. So I guess in the end the most sensible idea is to say nothing and hope for better than I know is true.

Author of *The Jaguar Hunter, Kalimantan, Life during Wartime . . .*

Paula Volsky

WHEN I WAS A CHILD, I enjoyed reading fairy tales and adventure yarns, for the sake of their color and excitement. (Why do I suspect that about 90 percent of the writers in this book are going to begin with similar if not identical comments?) I also enjoyed writing my own stories, partly for entertainment, and partly because an assortment of adults assured me that I did it well. I was a glutton for praise, back then.

Some things don't change.

The decades have passed. The short fairy tales of youth have given way to the comparative sophistication of fantasy novels. The adventure has remained pretty much the same in spirit, with improvements (I hope) in concept and execution. I still write for entertainment, for ego-gratification, and, these days, for money.

The work has its drawbacks. It is difficult and demanding. It is unlikely to furnish financial security. It is not for the lazy or the faint of heart. Some days, when the cursor on the blank screen blinks its relentless message, (go, go, GO) and my head is empty of words, I consider the disturbing alternative. If I weren't a professional writer, I might have to find a job and earn an honest living.

Author of *Illusion, The Gates of Twilight, The Wolf of Winter* . . .

Edward Whittemore

Edward Whittemore passed away.

Author of *Sinai Tapestry, Jerusalem Poker, Nile Shadows* . . .

Morgan Llywelyn

ALL FICTION IS, IN A SENSE, FANTASY. The writer of fiction creates a world that has never been and peoples it with characters according to the needs of the story. The world and the characters may or may not be based on reality, but they are always sculpted by the writer's mind. So whether the result is a reworking of ancient mythology or an up-to-the-minute police procedural thriller, any work of fiction depicts an alternate reality.

Irish writers, influenced by our Celtic heritage, are more familiar than most with the concept of alternate reality. For the Celts, the dividing line has always been very thin. In the Celtic cosmos, the Otherworld lies just beneath the surface of perceived reality and can break through at any time.

As a writer, my work falls into two broad categories. I established myself by writing mainstream, meticulously researched historical novels about Ireland and the Celts. But because fantasy is an alternative reality to Celts, no serious novel attempting accurately to depict their culture can ignore that element. As time passed, more and more of Celtic and Irish myth interjected itself into my work.

With a power all its own, fantasy broke through the surface of my perceived reality.

I still write mainstream historical novels, but in addition I now also write fantasy novels. And like my Celtic ancestors, sometimes I am not sure where the dividing line is.

Creativity depends upon a wellspring of imaginative energy. Writing fantasy allows that energy to flow free, to assume any form and follow any direction. The unfettered nature of speculative fiction is both a delight and a stimulus. "What if . . . ?" the fantasy writer asks. That one question is the perfect starting point for any writer: What if?

Fantasy is not merely a "genre," that denigrating term. Fantasy is a pinnacle, a mountaintop from which all horizons can be seen.

Author of Lion of Ireland, Bard, Brian Boru . . .

Bruce Coville

ONE OF THE THINGS that fantasy does best is create a sense of enchanted places, often in the form of a forest. (How I longed to walk among the trees of Middle Earth!)

I was lucky enough to grow up out in the country, in a house that had a lawn that sloped down to a swamp, which was followed by a field, which was followed by a forest. That wooded area always carried a sense of magic for me—a rich, deep, fulfilling magic that I often find myself trying to recapture in my fiction.

Author of *Goblins in the Castle, My Teacher Is an Alien, Eyes of the Tarot* . . .

Jennifer Roberson

HOT. BLINDING-BRIGHT. The acrid taste of caliche and alkali dust; the pungency of creosote and sage; transient shade and shadows beneath thorny mesquite umbrellas and the draperies of palo verde, weeping yellow blooms.

Ancient mountains stooped in the shoulders, sharpness rubbed away so the slopes are folded, crumbly. Desert colors: raisin, dusty purple, ashen sienna, cinnabar, ocher and amber and olive, a touch of acid green. Aglitter with mica, showing old bones of milky quartz, slick with hard-angled shale, shaped of granite clusters and porous lava rock spewed out by vanished volcanoes.

Horseback, bareback, barefoot. Out and away: under and through the squared-off arch of the old cavalry "fort," built for tenderfoot tourists; beyond the knobbed rails of the pens, alleys, corrals: wood cribbed away over years, sculpted by strong equine teeth into scallops, divots, islands.

Sorrel horse: copper-and-liver in the sunshine, bound only by bit, bridle, and reins. No saddle, no blanket, no pad, just slick ruddy horsehair raising sweat and salt in the heat. A big horse, high on the day and high-headed, snuffy, snorty, making me what cowboys call a "basketball" of his back: hunched and humpy statement of personal philosophy.

Then he eases, dribbles away the basketball; is silk now, moving easily, settling into the ride. Down over the scarp of the edge of arroyo, the lumpy vertebral trail cutting around jungles of knee-high sage, treacherous cholla, the squat, hydrantlike barrel cactus, fanned collections of prickly pear; dodging the stiff and ribby octopus limbs of spike-sheathed ocotillo.

Into the arroyo, dangerous in summer rains called monsoon; now dry, a desert glacier of sand and dirt, the jumbled jigsaw of river rocks tumbled smooth in once-rushing water. Life abounds: chipmunks, mice, lizards, a long-eared jackrabbit bounding away; the dry raspy buzz of a solitary rattlesnake tucked up in a rocky pocket to wait out the heat of the day. Overhead: a red-tailed hawk, carving lazy coilings against the sky.

It is a harsh beauty, a hard and sharp and desolate beauty made not of Eastern greens and crushed-velvet grass; of Midwestern yellows called corn and wheat; of the kudzu jungles of the South; or the rain-washed Northwest blue-and-pewter. This is the desert of the great Southwest, shaped of diversity, of *ad*versity, and a trilogy of cultures: Anglo, Hispanic, Indian.

This is Arizona. Hot and blinding-bright. Tasting of caliche and alkali, of creosote and sage, of horsehair and sweat and salt.

Out here in the desert, ahorse, beneath the sweet and singular coilings of a red-tailed raptor, one is aware of infinity.

That imagination is tangible, and all dreams possible.

Author of Lady of the Forest, Sword Bringer, A Pride of Princes . . .

George R. R. Martin

THE BEST FANTASY is written in the language of dreams. It is alive as dreams are alive, more real than real . . . for a moment at least . . . that long magic moment before we wake.

Fantasy is silver and scarlet, indigo and azure, obsidian veined with gold and lapis lazuli. Reality is plywood and plastic, done up in mud brown and olive drab. Fantasy tastes of *habañeros* and honey, cinnamon and cloves, rare red meat and wines as sweet as summer. Reality is beans and tofu, and ashes at the end. Reality is the strip malls of Burbank, the smokestacks of Cleveland, a parking garage in Newark. Fantasy is the towers of Minas Tirith, the ancient stones of Gormenghast, the halls of Camelot. Fantasy flies on the wings of Icarus, reality on Southwest Airlines. Why do our dreams become so much smaller when they finally come true?

We read fantasy to find the colors again, I think. To taste strong spices, and hear the songs the sirens sang. There is something old and true in fantasy that speaks to something deep within us, to the child who dreamed that one day he would hunt the forests of the night, and feast beneath the hollow hills, and find a love to last forever somewhere south of Oz and north of Shangri-La.

They can keep their heaven. When I die, I'd sooner go to Middle Earth.

Author of *Fevre Dream, Sandkings, The Armageddon Rag* . . .

106

Melanie Rawn

A COUSIN, hefting one of my tomes for the first time, asked, "How can you write such *long* books?" I replied, "You know how nobody in this family ever shuts up? Well, I just never shut up on paper, either."

My family says I haven't been shutting up since I was about three years old, when it seems I began my career as a teller of tales. Once, upon concluding one of these infant extravaganzas, I'm told that I looked solemnly up at the indulgent adults and confided, "But it's not *real*, you know."

No, it's not real. What fantasy writers do is play Make-Believe for a living. Put another way, we *make belief*. Which may mean that we never grow up (or shut up)—and probably don't particularly want to.

Author of *Dragon Prince, Stronghold, Skybowl* . . .

Peter David

MY ONGOING AMBITION in my writing has been to avoid typecasting. To that end, I've tried my hand at an assortment of venues, each with its own challenges, rewards, and drawbacks. There are two constants, though, in whatever area I've involved myself. The first is presenting stories and characters that view the world in a somewhat skewed manner. Since writers tend to use pieces of themselves in creating their protagonists and antagonists (else they risk creating ciphers), I suppose this is largely unavoidable.

The second is always to try to do the unexpected. To present something that will ideally make the reader stop, pause, and think about what he or she is seeing. As our lives become increasingly chaotic and frenzied, and information is sliced through with buzzsaw speed, that goal becomes an increasingly greater challenge. When one is using art to make a statement, one sometimes has to resort to radical means to do so.

I call this latest venture "Hiding Behind a Substantial Body of Work." And if there's any one message in my endeavors, it's the age-old one: Screw 'em if they can't take a joke.

Author of Howling Mad, Imzadi, Sachs & Violens . . .

Emma Bull

IT'S HARD TO TAKE a genuinely inclusive photograph of a writer. One needs at least a wide-angle lens, or one of those cameras that takes a panoramic photo; in the most dramatic cases, a helicopter shot is the only solution.

Writers will tell you they practice a lonely art, best accomplished in solitude. Rubbish. They may do the actual deed in private, closing out the flesh-and-blood presence of their fellows. But they couldn't do it—and might not even have *thought* of doing it—without the kindly influence of hordes of people, all of whom stand at their elbows in ghost-form forever after, watching the sentences take shape and laughing at the jokes. Family members show up in the crowd, and teachers from every level of education. There are lots of librarians hobnobbing there, many friendly bookstore clerks, and occasional tour guides from strange places. Other writers make up a large and noisy section of the party. Some of those are good friends, trusted workshoppers and commenters, long-suffering students. Some are the authors of books that (whether by good example or bad) made a difference. Then there are the musicians, artists, scientists, architects, gangsters, politicians, philosophers, race car drivers, telephone salespeople, and gas station attendants who inspired the words, or enriched them, or made it possible to stumble through the business of real life while writing them.

Consequently, sensible photographers avoid the problem. "I'm only taking a picture of you, the one who types the word," they'll say. "If you want a decent portrait of all those other people, you can do it yourself."

So the writer goes home and, adding the photographer to the helpful phantom crowd, writes another book.

Author of *The War for the Oaks, Finder, Bone Dance* . . .

Mercedes Lackey

A LOT OF MY LIFE seems to be involved with birds; Larry Dixon (my husband, cowriter and first editor as well as illustrator) was the one who first piqued my interest in them. Together we are federally licensed bird-of-prey rehabilitators as well as apprentice falconers, and have collected something of a menagerie of captive-bred parrots. Birds play a significant part in our work as well; there are the obvious symbolic aspects involved, such as freedom and fragility, and there are some symbolic aspects that are not so obvious.

We see birds—both in real life and fiction—as representative of responsibility. When we take on a parrot, we become responsible not only for its care, but for its well-being, both physical, emotional, and mental, for parrots are extremely intelligent and empathic creatures. When we take in an injured or orphaned raptor, we are often trying to undo what other people have done, either to the bird or to its environment.

And when we are entrusted with a parrot or a raptor, we accept the responsibility of *paying forward*. There is no way that anyone can ever pay back the good things that have come to them, so the only possible response to favors or good fortune is to pay *forward*, to give of yourself to the next need. Whether that is paying forward by spending countless hours tending to the needs of an orphaned hawk, or helping a new writer with his craft, we pay into the future in gratitude for our past.

Author of *Winds of Fate, Magic's Pawn, Sacred Ground . . .*

Phyllis Eisenstein

I NEVER INTENDED to be a fantasy writer. Rather, my goal, from the age of eight, was to be a science fiction writer, thereby writing in the genre I loved best. But I always enjoyed fantasy. Some of my earliest reading was of the Andrew Lang color-coded fairy tale books, which led me on to Grimm, Perrault, and others. And by the time I was ten or eleven, I had read most of Edgar Allan Poe's fiction, which made for an interesting balance. I was reading the science fiction magazines and the Groff Conklin anthologies by then, and it was becoming clear to me that science fiction and fantasy were a continuum—a spectrum, with SF at the violet end, fantasy at the red end, and a whole array of hard-to-categorize stories in the middle.

When an old *Twilight Zone* TV show came on the air, I saw that it spanned that spectrum, and it confirmed my feeling that there were no hard and fast barriers, that I could write in any color of the spectrum and still be in the same universe. One result of that feeling is that some of my stories are those hard-to-categorize creatures, those in-betweeners that might be science fiction or might be fantasy. But some are solidly in the fantasy end of the spectrum. With all that material from the Western European folkloric tradition absorbed in my formative reading years, it was almost inevitable that some fantasy ideas would leap out of my imagination and demand to be put down on paper. Important human questions were explored in that folkloric tradition—including questions of morality, identity, loyalty, compulsion—and they remain worth exploring, whether in a traditional, a modern, or a futuristic context.

My own work in the fantasy arena tends to focus on the problems of individuals rather than on world-spanning events. I am interested in the outsider, the alienated, the reluctant sorcerer, the seeker of a lost heritage—people searching for their places in the scheme of things, and for whatever happiness they can snatch from an indifferent universe. My stories also frequently concern the lust for power, and the sense of responsibility that must contend with it, the perils of obsessive hatred, and the emptiness of revenge. At least, these things can be found in my work. All of these aspects of the human condition speak to me much more strongly than any supposed struggle between abstract Good and Evil, so I leave that "larger canvas" to others.

Author of Sorcerer's Son, The Crystal Palace, Born to Exile . . .

Patricia A. McKillip

I WRITE FANTASY because it's there. I have no other excuse for sitting down for several hours a day indulging my imagination. Daydreaming. Thinking up imaginary people, impossible places. Imagination is the golden-eyed monster that never sleeps. It must be fed; it cannot be ignored. Making it tell the same tale over and over again makes it thin and whining; its scales begin to fall off; its fiery breath becomes a trickle of smoke. It is fed best by reality, an odd diet for something nonexistent; there are few details of daily life and its broad range of emotional context that can't be transformed into food for the imagination. It must be visited constantly, or else it begins to become restless and emit strange bellows at embarrassing moments; ignoring it only makes it grow larger and noisier. Content, it dreams awake, and spins the fabric of tales. There is really nothing to be done with such imagery except to use it: in writing, in art. Those who fear the imagination condemn it: something childish, they say, something monsterish, misbegotten. Not all of us dream awake. But those of us who do have no choice.

Author of *The Forgotten Beasts of Eld, Riddlemaster of Hed, The Book of Atrix Wolfe . . .*

John Lee

"WHAT IN THE WORLD are you going to do with a degree in Medieval History?" a friend of mine at Cambridge asked as we were about to graduate. "Not exactly useful in today's marketplace, is it?" No and yes. No, it didn't help me get a job—I went into advertising and thence into the film business. Yes, it has been enormously useful in fleshing out my fantasy writing. Research holds no terrors, indeed it keeps the necessity of actually getting down to the writing at bay.

An inclination toward history isn't the only component in the writing of fantasy, though it provided a spur for me. When I was nine, a classmate complimented me on my "furtive" imagination. I was as drunk on words as he was, but sober enough to know what he meant. That imagination, and the appreciation of the imagination of others, made me into a voracious reader of science fiction and of fantasy. When I felt the compulsion to write, an ascientific mind combined with a love of language and an affection for things medieval made fantasy an obvious choice.

Once started, I discovered the pleasure of creating worlds and people to live in them. I wasn't prepared, however, for my characters to develop wills of their own and start arguing with their creator, or for the fact that these "discussions" can take place away from the typewriter. I am now learning to cope with a reputation for eccentricity. The townsfolk smile compassionately and put it down to advancing age. I, of course, ascribe it to a "furtive" imagination at work.

Author of The Unicorn War, The Unicorn Quest, The Unicorn Peace . . .

Peter S. Beagle

A CHARACTER in one of my novels, a musician, says at one point, "The music was the only thing that ever came easily. Everything else I had to learn." That's as much of an autobiography as I'm ever likely to write.

I came by this thing I do honestly, even inevitably. My father was a natural storyteller; my mother loved all literature and read aloud to my brother and me every night. My parents remember me as a bouncy, sociable, talkative small child, in love with words and tales very early on, who only became shy and solitary somewhere around the time I learned to read. After that it was all up. That was truly all I wanted to do—the one frequently sliding into the other, as happens often even now—and however much my parents worried about their weird, overweight, antisocial kid, *they never said*. Not to me, anyway. However displaced I felt on the street, I always knew that my mother and father thought I was special. You can't buy that. There isn't a catalog house or credit card in the world that will give you *special*.

So. I'm fifty-seven years old. I'm married to the one person I ever wanted to be married to, who also happens to be the one other person I would wish to write like, if I could. I have three tender, honorable children. I'm a good writer—not great—I know what great is—but bloody good. What else? I do what I do. I tell stories and sing songs.

Author of *The Last Unicorn, A Fine and Private Place, The Innkeeper's Song . . .*

Pamela Dean

WRITERS ARE CHRONICALLY AFFLICTED with the impulse to complete the sentence, "Writing is like X." Being a stubbornly intuitive writer and a dilatory and intermittent gardener, I've settled on "planting a garden." It does well enough. Research is like those pleasing evenings spent during the Minnesota winter, poring over garden catalogs and planning gardens that will not survive in one's agricultural zone, require more physical labor than one has ever expended in one's life, or are likely to succumb in five minutes to one's local pests.

When Patti Perret took that picture, it was early May. You can see from the state of the spirea bushes and the vines of the Virginia creeper that it had been a long, cold spring. The weather was not encouraging to dilatory gardeners, except during two brief periods when I was elsewhere.

I didn't plant anything. Such perennials as I possess are almost all spring bloomers. When they were done flowering—a task they accomplished with unbecoming haste in the hot days of June—the wild campanula, the thistle, and the dandelion took over, just until ragweed, motherwort, and the tremendous towering wild mustard could relieve them. The raspberries, which had always objected to our neighbor's plan to let a mad hedge of fortuitous saplings grow up between his yard and ours, sprawled out of their shady bed and grew in the sunny lawn. Then the bindweed covered everything. Bindweed has smaller leaves than kudzu, but has much the same demoralizing effect on anybody who prefers a garden to a wilderness.

The red lilies I'd planted for my husband didn't come back. The seeds of native Minnesota wildflowers my girlfriend and I had bought at the state fair stayed in their yellow packets, as the weeds grew up and up and the bindweed covered the spirea bushes and the Virginia creeper engulfed the sidewalk.

The book I'm writing this year is far too much like this. It's my own fault. The book is based on Child Ballad No. 1, which in some of its versions has a pleasant botanical chorus: Juniper, gentian, and rosemary. I called the book after it. This is known as asking for trouble.

The book was tame at first, like the perennials. But once they had bloomed obediently in the first chapters, strange shoots from out of my past, old memories long buried, new seeds of plants I'm not used to, all came up like the wild mustard and the bindweed and those furry blue flowers on long runners that grow in the cracks of the driveway.

The perennials are still there underneath: shiny peony leaves, toppling blades of the daylily, unblooming mounds of the bleeding-heart, drooping forget-me-nots all gone to seed, indefatigable mint making itself known, though not seen, whenever I mow the lawn.

They define the garden, but this year, they are not the garden. And I have an unfinished novel full of wild mustard and leafed all over with bindweed.

Author of *Tam Lin, The Secret Country, The Dubious Hills* . . .

124

Terry Pratchett

ONCE, when I was learning my trade as a newspaper reporter, I had to interview a famous footballer (famous, at least, in our small town—and by football I of course mean proper *English* football). The sports editor had given me a list of important questions to ask, all about technique and approach.

I asked them. The footballer, a man of skilled feet but limited education, did his best for a while to answer them and then said, "Look, it's like this. I get the ball, and I does me best to get it into the goal. I can't tell you how I do it. You clever buggers should be the ones tellin' *me* how I do it. I just *do* it."

Later on, I worked out what he meant. He meant you shouldn't ask the sculptor how he works out which bits of stone aren't statue. You shouldn't ask the man on the tightrope how he keeps his balance. You can ask the writer why he or she writes. But I'm not sure the answer will be any more coherent, although it will contain far more words, and I'll keep mine short.

All I know is that I've always written the Discworld books for fun, and was lucky enough to come up with a world that is flexible enough to more or less accommodate anything I want to write; I started off by parodying post-Tolkien fantasy and have more or less ended up parodying real life. I don't ever remember sitting down and planning the whole thing. It always seemed like a good idea at the time. I'm having a lot of fun and people keep giving me money. I'm not supposed to say no, am I?

Author of the Discworld books, Book of the Nomes series, *The Carpet People* . . .

Ellen Kushner

WHEN I WAS A KID, reading books made me happier than anything. So I believed that the people who were privileged to write those books must be a celestial choir of chosen beings, happy all the time. I thought this was a fine aspiration, and set out to become a writer.

In my twenties, my first short story sale gave me three hours of dancing-on-the-ceiling elation, followed by grim dejection when I realized that I was just going to have to do it all over again.

So I did it again, and again, and I published novels, and people even liked them. It was then that I discovered the terrible truth:

I still had to do my own laundry.

Yes, I was a real writer at last, but the dishes continued to pile up in the sink. And where were the beautiful men in tuxedos with the champagne? I'd been so sure that they were part of the package.

It was not all that long ago that I realized I was going to have to write them into my life myself. And so I have. I only hope that someone, somewhere, is reading one of my books, and that, for the moment, it is making them happier than anything.

Author of *Swordspoint, Thomas the Rhymer* . . .

Neil Gaiman

THESE ARE NOT OUR FACES.

This is not what we look like.

You think Gene Wolfe looks like his photograph in this book? Or Jane Yolen? Or Peter Straub? Or Diana Wynne Jones? Not so. They are wearing play-faces to fool you. But the play-faces come off when the writing begins.

Frozen in black and silver for you now, these are simply masks. We who lie for a living are wearing our liar-faces, false-faces made to deceive the unwary. We must be—for, if you believe these photographs, we look just like everyone else.

Protective coloration, that's all it is.

Read the books: sometimes you can catch sight of us in there. We look like gods and fools and bards and queens, singing worlds into existence, conjuring something from nothing, juggling words into all the patterns of night.

Read the books. That's when you see us properly: naked priestesses and priests of forgotten religions, our skins glistening with scented oils, scarlet blood dripping down from our hands, bright birds flying out from our open mouths. Perfect, we are, and beautiful in the fire's golden light. . . .

There was a story I was told as a child, about a little girl who peeked in through a writer's window one night, and saw him writing. He had taken his false-people-face off to write and had hung it behind the door, for he wrote with his real face on. And she saw him; and he saw her. And, from that day to this, nobody has ever seen the little girl again.

Since then, writers have looked like other people even when they write (though sometimes their lips move, and sometimes they stare into space longer, and more intently, than anything that isn't a cat); but their words describe their real faces: the ones they wear underneath.

This is why people who encounter writers of fantasy are rarely satisfied by the wholly inferior persons that they meet.

"I thought you'd be taller, or older, or younger, or prettier, or wiser," they tell us, in words or wordlessly.

"This is not what I look like," I tell them. "This is not my face."

Author of The Sandman, Angels and Visitations, Miracle Man . . .

Robert Holdstock

IF MYTHOLOGY AND LEGEND evolved by use of imagination to explain the strangeness of nature, the mystery of our origins, the unexplainable in the world around us, then both myth and legend, and imagination *itself* contain clues to worlds now lost, heroes now forgotten, lands and insights now obscure.

The hunting of these forgotten realms and heroes gives me great pleasure; thinking I've found any one of them exhilarates me.

Imagination, if used carefully, is a time machine of great value, and I have been traveling in time since I was a child. It is also wonderful for papering over the cracks in reality!

Author of Mythago Wood, Lvondyss, The Fetch . . .

Elizabeth Moon

GROWING UP MARGINAL in the 1950s—socially, as a child of divorce, an only child, a girl with unsuitable interests; geographically, at the southern tip of Texas, 250 miles south of San Antonio—had advantages for a future SF/F writer. Those who've grown up marginal find the edges of things—from forests to cultures—ideal habitat. Writing science fiction and fantasy lets me use what I am.

Author of *The Deed of Paksenarrion, Surrender None, Liar's Oath . . .*

Terry Goodkind

SOME OF MY EARLIEST MEMORIES are of people who lived in my head. I didn't think of them coming from stories I made up, but as characters in great emotional turmoil telling me their tales each night as I went to sleep.

I have a form of dyslexia that makes me misinterpret words, so I'm a slow reader because I have to work at reading words correctly. From the beginning, teachers chastised me because they thought I wasn't trying. That I understood what I read was apparently of no importance. They seemed to value quantity over quality; to me, that eviscerated the story. Reading for school became a form of punishment.

I started going off to the library and reading adventure stories. I loved being taken away to far-off places; the words created a special reality in my mind, the way my bedtime characters did. It never occurred to me that other people felt the same way when they read. To me, it was a very secret thrill; it was magic.

I knew very well that what I was reading was not the kind of thing I was supposed to be reading. I had been taught that it was only right to read incredibly boring things. Reading was a chore; this stuff was fun.

As time went on, every English class I had drove home the point that reading was not to be enjoyed, that in what you wrote, the story was irrelevant—that only the technical aspects mattered. I wrote stories all the time, but only in my head. If nobody saw them, they couldn't rebuke my private stories, which I loved.

Years later, when I was a high school senior, my English teacher was Mrs. Hansen, and she really made a difference. She told me that there was something beyond the mechanics of writing that was profoundly important. She encouraged me to write *stories;* let me touch something noble.

She didn't care how long it took me to read; she just wanted to know what I thought about the stories, the characters, the emotion. She made it okay for me to read for the sheer joy of it. She was a hand in the darkness. Suddenly, the experience of writing gave me the same joy of the worlds I discovered when I was younger. It was an alternate reality: magic. It was then that I knew I would someday be a writer. It was a secret, private dream, but I knew.

Writing is magic for me. Maybe that's why I feel such a deep connection to fantasy, to magic. I think that back then in Mrs. Hansen's class, when I harbored the secret that someday I would be a writer, one other person knew my secret.

Author of Wizard's First Rule, Stone of Tears, Blood of the Fold . . .

Nancy Springer

I AM TRYING TO WRITE, but I am facing a mirror and the woman in the mirror is getting in my way; I must move to a different chair. There, that's better. The person in the mirror, that woman—middle-aged, graying, round-faced, round all over—that was me okay, yet it could not be the writer. Looking at her, I could not write. The writer is a young thing, a fresh thing, a tadpole thing, not that frog in the mirror.

I am an ambling, puffing person with asthma, but the writer is a butterfly on a summer breeze.

I am a gnome with nose hair and wax in my ears, but the writer is all eyes and antennae, almost faceless, a sprite, an elf.

I am wearing my favorite fuzzy sweater, but the writer dances naked.

I curl lumpen in a chair, but the writer runs, races, swims, flies, radiates, emanates, creates.

I get up, walk outside, cross the street to the convenience store for some powdered doughnuts. The writer is watching through my eyes, a shackled angel living in darkness, looking to the light.

I will grow old and get arthritis and wear ugly shoes with Odor-Eaters in them and my asthma will get worse and one way or another I will die. I have no trouble whatsoever believing this. But I cannot believe that the writer will ever die.

Author of *Larque on the Wing, Metal Angel, The Red Wizard* . . .

Kara Dalkey

GROWING UP PAINFULLY SHY gave me the outlook of being somewhat alien from the rest of the human species. I have been drawn to such studies as history, anthropology, archaeology, and mythology to try to learn why people do what they do and believe what they believe. Reading history showed me that the variety of human behavior and belief in past societies is far greater than any fictional world I could invent. So I tend to set my fantasy novels and stories within a specific historical setting, suffused with the fascinating creatures of that era or location's mythology and folktale. I'm not sure that I've come to understand humanity any better, but I'm having a good time writing stories.

And now and then I like to write humorous and silly things, because life is too bizarre to take it too seriously.

Author of *The Nightingale, The Curse of Sagamore, Goa . . .*

Lisa Tuttle

FANTASY, TO ME, is about people and their inner worlds. Fantasy itself—the human need for and use of it—interests me; inventing or taking part in role-playing games does not. What I find especially compelling is that ambiguous, murky, and dangerous region where the very things we fear the most are also those we secretly desire. I write in search of knowledge lost in childhood and the sinister clarity of dreams.

Author of *Dreamhaven*, "The Bone Flute," "Stranger in the House" . . .

Diane Duane and Peter Morwood

DUANE: People get ideas about the life of a fantasy writer, especially when the writer lives in Ireland. They get all rhapsodic about the beautiful scenery, and how it must help your work to be in such a romantic country.

Not true. A recent work day went this way: Get up, feed cats, eat breakfast. (One hour.) Start writing. (Ten minutes.) Postman arrives, gossip ensues, start work again. (Twenty minutes.) Phone rings thrice in succession: conversations with French, German, and British producers. (Fifty minutes.) Cats shed on desk. Remove cats. Several times. (Twenty minutes.) Start writing again. (Six minutes.) Federal Express arrives. Gossip. (Ten minutes.)

(Sigh.) Start writing again. (One hour fifteen minutes.) Pause on hearing odd sound outside. Discover forty of the neighbor's sheep loose and eating potted plants. Run outside to remove sheep. Several times. (Two hours.) Phone rings again. (Fifteen minutes.) Go back outside, remove sheep some more. Pitch fit over now-defoliated rosemary bush. Vow to find and eat guilty sheep. (One hour.) Husband gets up (having been up working till 5:00 A.M.), we talk. (Twenty minutes.)

Start writing again. (Thirty minutes.) Phone calls: among them, neighbor needing recipe for Women's Institute project (suggest Sheep Rosemary). (One hour.) Back to desk: writing again. (One hour.) Run out of steam. Eat dinner, watch news, collapse. (Two hours.)

My days have been like that for the past eight years. Now you know why *The Door into Starlight* is so late. . . . But Ireland *is* very pretty. . . .

MORWOOD: I wanna tell you a story. That's why I write. To entertain both thee and me.

Writing fantasy is like writing anything else. You have to get it right, or at least convincing. Sometimes it's looking sideways at Real History (whatever that is). Maybe it's a history you made up, or maybe it's the modern world two over.

But fantasy can be decked out with other things that might not fit in a more limited genre: the glass towers of Manhattan backlit by a thermonuclear sunset; the delight of "faraway places with strange-sounding names." Places where fleas never bite, the camel never spits, and the food is invariably good—unless written otherwise for effect.

My hobbies get in there; the obvious ones for a fantasy writer: from history, weapons, costume, travel, etc., and the less obvious, like cooking. The enjoyment of food and drink encourages reader-character identification like nothing else.

As Kingsley Amis pointed out, a feast should make the reader want to be there. I once produced what one editor still calls "the high dribble factor," brought on by reading a lovingly described banquet scene—followed by the realization that it's two hours before lunch.

So be warned. And make a sandwich. . . .

Duane is the author of *The Door into Fire, So You Want to Be a Wizard?, Deep Wizardry* . . . Morwood is the author of *Firebird, Warlord's Domain, Widowmaker* . . .

James P. Blaylock

I WROTE MY FIRST SHORT STORY in the fifth grade, and it happened that it was a fantasy story. A friend had told me about a film he'd seen, entitled (apparently) *Macabre,* which I naturally assumed was meant as a name, probably spelled McCob. So I wrote a story in which a family is terrorized in a farmhouse by a skeleton with this same name, wearing a straw hat and smoking a corncob pipe. Beyond that I can't remember a lot about the story, whether McCob murdered the family or they drove him away or just what. I can remember, though, that I thought the whole thing was pretty funny, especially the notion of such an unlikely and ridiculous name. I was off and running with that story, and I never looked back, and these thirty-five years later I realize that my work has consistently mined those same oddball themes — the pipe, the funny hat, the ridiculous name, the malevolent skeleton — and that publishers have *paid* me for it, and my stories have been translated into foreign languages so that Italian people and Portuguese people and Swedes can all be exposed to these things, and as far as I'm concerned it's great to be alive, and the world is a far stranger place than any of us fantasy writers give it credit for.

Author of *Homunculus, Lord Kelvin's Machine, The Last Coin . . .*

146

Susan Cooper

THE WORLD IS ITSELF so astonishing that it seems strange some of us should be driven to invent creatures and stories even more fantastical than those around us. As a writer, I'm a jack-of-all-trades: journalist, novelist, playwright, screenwriter. But whenever my imagination can run free, unencumbered by facts or commissions, the stories that it brings me always seem to be fantasies, generally of a sort published these days as novels for children. Perhaps writers of my kind are able to tell the truth only through metaphor. Or perhaps we're just greedy, wanting always not only to look in the mirror but to step through it, not only to live today but, to fly in and out of yesterday and tomorrow. "This is how life is," says the realistic novel. The fantasy says, "Yes, but what if—?" So the writer picks up his pen and begins. "In a hole in the ground there lived a hobbit. . . ."

Author of *Mandrake, The Dark Is Rising, Over Sea under Stone* . . .

Joan Aiken

I HAVE ALWAYS BEEN INTERESTED in the way that elements of stories twine and combine. At school I had an art teacher, a great influence on me, who disliked man-made objects unless they were old and showed the effects of time and wear; she loved all natural things. I share this attitude and it plays a large part in my writing. I'm fascinated by the ambiguity of man's relationship to the huge, mysterious universe around him; how, on the one hand, we make ourselves little boxes and think to exist safely and snugly in them; on the other, we extend our knowledge further and further into the limitless void; and yet from time to time these opposites collide and produce astonishing results.

Author of *The Wolves of Willoughby Chase, Give Yourself a Fright, The Cockatrice Boys . . .*

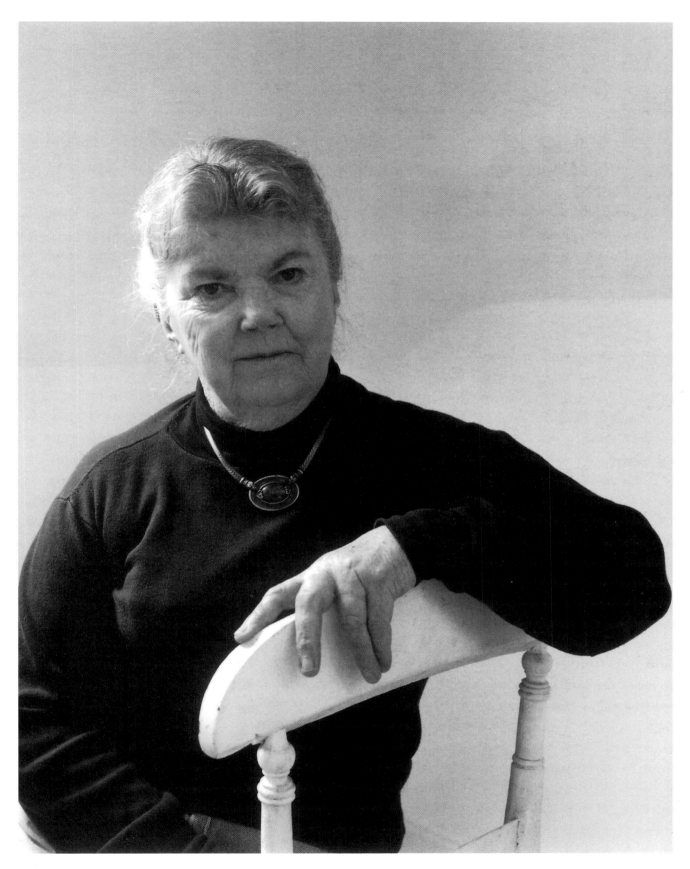

L. Sprague de Camp

I'VE BEEN WRITING professionally for a little over sixty years and I've written in a number of different fields. About half my output has been fiction and the other half has been nonfiction.

The fiction has been nearly all science fiction or fantasy, although I have published several historical novels. The historical novels were kindly received by the critics.

Unfortunately, I started in this genre just as it began its decline from its peak of popularity in the 1950s. Hence, each novel sold fewer copies than its predecessor. When the last of the five, *The Golden Wind,* followed this precedence, although I considered it the best of the lot, I said, "to hell with this nonsense," and went back to science fiction and fantasy.

In nonfiction, I have been published mainly as a science writer—a popularizer of science news, generally. I also wrote for over a year a series of scripts for delivery on radio, a weekly science broadcast. In this work, I have had to range over the entire fields of science and technology.

My favorite scientific subjects, however, have been in the biological and anthropological and geological fields. The sciences having to do with life on Earth such as geology, biology, paleontology, and anthropology. As a boy and a youth my great ambition was to be a paleontologist and to spend my life digging up the fossils of dinosaurs and other extinct forms of life. Parental influence pointed me in other directions, but I have been able, in my writing, to indulge myself in those fields.

My most recent hardcover book, *The Ape-Man Within,* is a speculation about the connection between the peculiar behavior of men in large numbers, as in nations, over millions of years of descent from ancestors who lived lives much like those of a modern chimpanzee band.

Despite all the hundreds of writings that I've had published, the things of which I am most proud are a couple of very minor discoveries or surmises that, professional friends in those fields tell me, I was apparently the first to make. One in the history of technology when I guessed the true function of an item of saddlery in classical art, and one concerning the function in life of a feature of the anatomy of certain dinosaurs.

Author of *Rogue Queen, Lest Darkness Falls,* coauthor (with Fletcher Pratt) of *The Incomplete Enchanter . . .*

Caroline Stevermer

I AM FINALLY LEARNING how to drive a car. After years of nervous reluctance, I had a few days in which I felt it might be possible to buy a car and learn to drive it. "If it isn't easy, it's impossible," that's what my mother always says. The corollary is that if it *is* easy, jump on it, because it won't be easy for long. The feeling passed, as I knew it would, but by the time it did, it was too late. I already owned a car and all the appurtenances: license, tabs, insurance, ice scraper, jumper cables, and most of all, a gigantic car loan.

I have already learned a lot from this experience, more than I would have, I think, if I'd been any use behind the wheel at the age of sixteen. For one thing, I've noticed driving has a few things in common with writing.

To learn to drive, you have to drive. Classes and books are important, but you can't learn it just by thinking about it. You have to actually do it. Unfortunately.

You can improve your driving through practice alone if you must, but with the right kind of coaching, you can become a better driver more quickly.

Some people start out with better cars. Some people never get the hang of parallel parking. Road conditions are subject to change. Objects in the mirror are closer than they appear. Your mileage may vary.

I am still, after trying hard almost every day for more than six months, quite nervous about driving and often reluctant to do so. I do it anyway. I've been writing since I was eight. I am still quite nervous about it and often reluctant to do so—but I try hard almost every day.

Author of *A College of Magicks, Serpent's Egg, River Rats* . . .

John M. Ford

How lovely that the chemistry of silver,
The metal already alloyed to fantasy,
Beloved of poets, should create a picture,
Like magic, as magic does, derailing Time
To salt down an expression in the flash,
Turning it face outward in the print.

It is not easier to hide oneself in print.
Although the words may slip by quick as silver,
Eye drawing mind toward a single cortical flash,
It takes many well-set hooks to suspend the fantasy,
A long baseline of revelations over time,
Phrases and clauses vignetting and dodging the picture.

Think of it as a puzzle, then, this picture.
What's behind those eyes, on the other side of
    the print?
Is the cloudy castle's drawbridge down this time,
Betrayed by the motor-driven pieces of silver?
What echo there to the grave dead call, Why fantasy?
What wings or claws will show up in the flash?

Isn't it sting how we hope to end in a flash,
One instant here, then there, however you may picture
There to be, let it be sudden, so runs the fantasy.
Give us our full stop, like a period in print,
And go as shining gold, not tarnished silver,
Posed on an overlook, set back from the cliffs of Time.

One way or other, it's all a deal with Time.
A dance of phosphenes from the One Great Flash,
Hydrogen galliards making nitrogen and silver,
Shadows that wish to cast a solid picture,
To walk all lightly and still leave a print—
Ah, Paradox, the spine of fantasy.

So here we are, snapping the mirror on fantasy,
Banking a bit of second-mortgaged time,
Nodding enough as not to flare the print,
Sitting in the purple twilight past the flash,
Trying to write a frame around the picture,
Recalling that there is no rhyme for silver.

Author of *The Dragon Waiting, The Princes of the Air, Web of Angels* . . .

156

Susan Shwartz

"YOU KNEW THE JOB WAS DANGEROUS when you took it."

The adage makes it sound as if I had a choice and a purpose in mind instead of a series of evolving needs.

I always wanted to search out a dragon's hoard of information. One Ph.D., thirteen years on Wall Street, and sixteen years (and counting, please God) in New York City, I find myself—information junkie, shoe- and workaholic, and culture-vulture—not guarding my hoard, but using it to build a series of increasingly incongruous bridges that strike me as sensible and necessary. A Jewish version of Wagner's *Parsifal* sells in Germany. A Nebula certificate for a story about Vietnam winds up at the Wall. And a cyberspace salon welcomes the widest assortment of visitors since *Star Wars*' Cantina with formal courtesy.

What I've learned about bridge building is that, just about the time you should be mortaring in the keystone (if those are the right terms), you run out of material. So you throw yourself across the span to complete the work. It puts you at the center, but perhaps not the way you had intended. This disconcerting, if satisfying, method of construction has made me, like one of Cordwainer Smith's Ladies of the Instrumentality, bitterly in favor of kindness.

Author of Shards of Empire, The Grail of Hearts, Silk Roads and Shadows . . .

158

C. J. Cherryh

THE ANCIENT WORLD WAS FULL OF MAGIC. Most everyone north and northwest of the Mediterranean believed that standing barefoot on the earth gave you special knowledge, that the prickling feeling at the back of your neck meant watchers in the woods, and that running water cleansed supernatural flaws.

True magic, magic as our ancestors practiced it, contained very little concept of good or evil as the modern world understands such terms. The ancient world understood powers, and Powers, and believed that if you should trespass beyond the natural and convenient boundaries of your birth and natural status, as very little prevents you from doing, you must enter into the natural and convenient boundaries of Something Else . . . which may resent your presence, may be curious about you, or may deal with you in ignorance perilous to both.

On the one hand, that ancient belief encouraged the timid to stay by their own firesides.

On the other, it placed no barriers of class or skill or gender between the adventuresome and adventure.

That was the real ancient world—a period in which I have some background. My study in university was the ancient Mediterranean, and that interest led me into both Egyptian and Celtic lore, which led . . . everywhere, ultimately.

What can the ancient world offer a modern world that has encroached so recklessly into the deep forests and the sea, and by ax and fire and iron brought the Powers of domestic fields up against those of the wild places?

It can offer encounter, strange meetings with the not-evil, not-good, and an examination of one's own actions.

It can teach one to look under bushes and beside trails, and to listen in the Wild and not chatter.

It can teach us what our ancestors knew: that you can't divide nature into good and evil, that you can't speak to the earth politely if you've only gone shod and on concrete, and that you can't know the wild countryside if you roar through it in glass and steel on asphalt ribbons.

The ancient world can teach us, too, as Virgil suggested, "Forsan et haec olim meminisse iuvabit," that adventures are most pleasant to contemplate not while rain is dripping down one's neck, but when one is safe and warm at home, and confident of supper.

Author of Gate of Ivrel, Morgaine, Well of Shiuan . . .

Steven Brust

THE PLAY OF TWO SMALL PAIR in draw poker is strongly dependent on position. If I'm sitting to the immediate left of the opener, I'll raise the limit and hope to drive out as many players as possible, whereas if I'm late after the opener, I might even fold, figuring my hand, probably the best before the draw, is unlikely to be the best after the draw. I rarely bluff a pat hand; I'd rather take my one-in-eleven shot at filling, because I don't mind folding one out and waiting until I'm fairly sure I have a hand that will run.

Writing? Yeah, I play that pretty much the same way.

Author of *Taltos, Jhereg, The Phoenix Guards* . . .

Suzy McKee Charnas

SOME OF US ARE LUCKY ENOUGH to get to fantasize openly, not to say brazenly, for our livelihood. Since childhood I've been drawn to reading and telling tales of the mythic and the weird—werewolves and Amazons, warriors and enchanters, or modern and ambiguous monsters like the witch who lives down your suburban street or the eons-old vampire who teaches anthropology in a small New England college—all denizens of the territory of the fabulous. In that sinister, luminous, and erotic country I'm a sketcher of venerable ruins, a quilter of patches cut from richer, older garments, and a shameless mixer of metaphors.

It's my passion to descend to the fifth cellar down for a taste of married life with the Phantom of the Opera; or to inhabit the mind of a sculptor in the future cutting Merlin out of the imprisoning tree; or to unlock the secret of a ghost from the days of the French Revolution (and, of course, to invite you along on my travels). The project of fantasy is above all collaborative, unfolding down generations and across cultures and media, which is both the root and the flower of its immense and irrepressible vitality.

Author of *The Vampire Tapestry, Walk to the End of the World, Dorothea Dreams* . . .

Harry Harrison

IT'S NOT A BAD LIFE, writing. Certainly writing science fiction and fantasy is a lot better than writing say, Romances or Westerns. Can you imagine going to a convention of Western readers? Everyone rolling cigarettes with one hand, hucksters selling spurs, six-shooters, mustache wax. The thought of attending a convention of Romance readers is just too horrible to imagine. Almost as unimaginable as a Barbara Cartland convention. No one under eighty need apply. Pages of pink Kleenex bound into every program book. No one admitted who does not wear triple strands of pearls. Forget that. I'll stick with the field I know. The writers are all good fun and they used to drink too much. Cigarette in one hand, strong whiskey in the other. All gone now. I like to talk to the fans too, although in England they smoke too much and in U.S. they eat too much. In Sweden they bore too much. In Italy they buy your books but have no desire to talk to you. I could tell you stories about Russian, Rumanian, Latvian fans that would make you blush. I will not. The good thing is that they all read my books and seem happy to do so. Can't complain about that. Thanks, readers; don't stop now.

Author of *The Hammer and the Cross, One King's Way, King and Emperor*...

Steve Stern

SOME YEARS AGO, I discovered quite accidentally that, when my grandparents came to this country, they brought a lot of baggage. They brought with them, along with various superstitions, an odd assortment of devils and angels, creatures native to their homeland—what the immigrants called "the other side." In the end, like everyone else, these creatures were assimilated into American life. Waiving all ethical standards, they took up with one another and with mortals, until human beings, devils, and angels became a single hybrid race in our streets. After only a couple of generations we even managed to forget that we were the spawn of such awful and wonderful unions; that we were the products of illicit mixed marriages between the celestial and the terrestrial (not to say infernal) realms; matches made between eternity and time. I don't know what good it does to recall one's impure origins, but speaking for myself, it's been some solace to think I must be more than meets the eye.

Author of *The Moon and Ruben Shein, Lazar Malkin Enters Heaven, A Plague of Dreamers* . . .

Judith Tarr

SO WHERE DOES FANTASY END and reality begin? Up here on the mesa under an endless southwestern sky, with a yardful of Lipizzans and whole regiments of dragons' teeth turning up underfoot, I honestly couldn't tell you.

The line between history and fantasy is even harder to trace. Write history as it was lived, thinking in the present tense, and you find yourself, if you're writing Egypt or Greece or China or, for that matter, the Yucatan or the Dreamtime, not only believing in magic but living and working it. So what is real, and what's imaginary? Is magic a lie or a different way to look at the truth? My publisher, as baffled as I am, finally took the word *fantasy* off the spine of one of my books and put on plain old *fiction* instead—and the book was nominated for the World Fantasy Award.

In the end, of course, it doesn't matter. What is, is. I just write what I see. Mostly it's a past so strange it seems fantastical. Once in a while it's a flash from an alternate present or an interstellar future. The magic varies, but it's always there. Like an ancient Egyptian or even the most rational Greek, I can't imagine the world without it.

Author of Arrows of the Sun, Alamut, Throne of Isis . . .

Katharine Kerr

PEOPLE OFTEN ASK ME if I'll write other fantasy novels someday that don't take place in the world of Deverry. At this point, the answer would be no, simply because Deverry has a lot of unanswered questions for me still. Of course, one never knows what one's unconscious mind has planned. Deverry itself was certainly a production of the Unconscious, in the Jungian sense. For a while, when the material seemed to be pouring itself onto the paper as I typed, I was calling myself "Archetypes R Us."

Various readers over the years have asked me where I "get my ideas." My answer is always "from the same place you get your dreams." Although all good fiction springs from the unconscious, nonrational parts of the mind, good fantasy in particular shares the urgency of dream and its sense of magical lands and endless possibilities. Fantasy writing, which draws on myths and legends for its inspiration, recounts what we might call the "recurring dreams of Western culture." The growing market for fantasy shows that these dreams are very much alive and potent today, no matter how "archaic" their trappings.

Author of Darkspell, A Time of Omens, The Bristling Wood *. . .*

Robert Jordan

ALL IS ILLUSION. You think that you have seen me? You have not.

I walk the jeweled jungles of the night, rarely padding the planes of sight. Mist curls from my nostrils when I lie in my badger's cave, fog carpeting the land, cloaking the mortal world. Fog, where fireflies dance for me alone, sculpting patterns inside my skull, and uncounted unknown glowing mites take on shape and flesh. Worlds and time spin beneath my hands, and threads of myth, writhing throughout the ages, weave themselves into dreams where mortal shadows shift among the darkling flames. Ancient tales that tug at souls, reminding the eyes of things unseen yet remembered. All dreams and fears and hungers are the same, a thousand times a thousand branches spreading, kindled from the same roots. One branch for another I change, graft the alien stock to germinate untold from native, 'round and down to where myth and dreams alike are born. Into the jeweled jungle, into the fog, where the fireflies dance.

Then again, maybe I just tell stories. All is illusion.

Author of The Eye of the World, The Dragon Reborn, Lord of Chaos . . .

Jane Yolen

FOR ME, the literature of the fantastic began with storytelling. After all, humans are the storytelling animal. Only now we do most of our storytelling on the page.

I am obsessed with stories—my own and other people's. I want my music and art to tell stories as well. *What happened next?* is probably the first sentence I ever spoke. And even if it isn't, I can certainly pretend it is since both my parents are no longer around to contradict me.

Everyone in my family was a storyteller. Some people called them liars. But the Yolen gene is a storytelling gene. And on it goes. My daughter writes, one son is a musician whose songs tell stories, the other a photographer who catches stories in his lens.

When I die, I want my tombstone to read: SHE WROTE MANY GOOD BOOKS AND ONE GREAT ONE. I will let the readers of that argue over which book I mean. That will force them to read the stories—and tell their own.

Author of *Briar Rose, Merlin's Booke*, the Great Alta sequence . . .

Craig Shaw Gardner

FANTASY, like all genre fiction, is often considered "escapist fare," but it has always seemed to me that you can learn something while you're escaping. After all, in fantastic fiction, just like in life, it's the stuff that sneaks up on you that can really whop you upside the head.

Author of A Malady of Magicks, The Last Arabian Night, Dragon Sleeping . . .

Jack Williamson

SOMEWHAT ISOLATED AS A CHILD, I've always lived in dreamland. A poor and narrow place at first, but enriched enormously when I discovered science fiction. That happened in 1926, back before it was named science fiction. Hugo Gernsback was still calling it "scientifiction," filling the early *Amazing Stories* with the reprinted classics of Jules Verne and H. G. Wells, A. Merritt, and Edgar Rice Burroughs. Captured instantly, I learned the laws of fantasy, learned to build better dreams of my own.

A literally fabulous land, but not always enough. Timidly at first, sometimes painfully, I ventured out into reality. Far enough to make loyal friends, to find a place in the congenial company of science fiction, finally to serve as a weather forecaster in World War II, to make a good marriage that lasted until Blanche's death in 1985, to become a college professor, to visit all the continents.

A great life, altogether, but dreamland is still the snug and pleasant place where I feel most at home. I've always been glad to get back to it, and happily surprised that the fountains of wonder have yet to fail.

Author of Darker Than You Think, Golden Blood, Demon Moon . . .

Lawrence Watt-Evans

Watt-Evans's First Law of Fantasy: Stories are about people.

Watt-Evans's Second Law of Fantasy: People are never wholly good or wholly evil, and therefore characters should never be wholly good or wholly evil.

Watt-Evans's Third Law of Fantasy: The basic human motivations are universal.

Watt-Evans's Fourth Law of Fantasy: Everything *other* than the basic human motivations will vary, depending on the cultural setting.

Watt-Evans's Fifth Law of Fantasy: Magic, like everything else, has rules.

Watt-Evans's Sixth Law of Fantasy: If a story can be written without a fantasy element, then don't bother with the fantasy element.

Author of *With a Single Spell, In the Empire of Shadow, The Lure of the Basilisk* . . .

Will Shetterly

IN FORTY YEARS, I have learned these things:

1. Art *is* the real world.
2. Take care of your teeth.
3. Organized religion is best left for organizations.
4. Politics is a dirty business, but if you do not do politics, politics will be done to you.
5. It is always necessary to be honest; it is never necessary to be cruel.

Author of *Cats Have No Lord, NeverNever, Witch Blood* . . .

Ru Emerson

WHEN I WAS GROWING UP, I always knew I'd do something creative, and writing was a strong contender (along with music, acting, opera, and dance), but until I discovered fantasy in my twenties, nothing clicked. There is probably no other genre that gives me such freedom to incorporate so much of myself in what I write: a strong interest in history, which contributes to any world I create; my childhood in western Montana and my present home in western rural Oregon, both of which are reflected in the importance of the land itself, the weather, climate, how they affect plot and characters. No other genre, certainly, in which I can look at anything from Shakespeare to the spread of the Huns in Europe to a ballet hosted by Kermit the Frog and think,

"What if . . . ?"—and have it become a story.

Author of *To the Haunted Mountains, Spell Bound, The Science of Power . . .*

187

Fred Saberhagen

I'VE BEEN ABLE TO SAY for many years now that the best job in the world is mine. And the number who can make that claim about their daily work is small indeed. Fantastic!

Author of *Empire of the East, An Old Friend of the Family,* the Book of Swords series . . .

Patricia C. Wrede

TECHNICALLY, ALL FICTION IS FANTASY. It hasn't happened in "real life"; it has been invented. But there is a divide between fantastic literature and other, more realistic fiction.

Most fiction is like a pane of glass, a window that we look through to see another view of the world outside ourselves. It is not a tale of real events, but it *looks* real. Fantastic literature is not merely not-real, it is *aggressively* not-real. The events in a fantasy novel are not simply things that *have* not happened; they are things that *cannot* happen. Dragons and unicorns exist only as metaphors, and the daylight world suffers a serious shortage of magic swords and flying carpets.

Thus, fantasy does something different from realistic mainstream and historical fiction. Fantasy takes the window and coats the outside with the silver of wondrous impossibilities—elves, dragons, wizards, magic. And the window becomes a mirror that reflects both ourselves and all the things in the shadows behind us, the things we have tried to turn our backs on. More: In the best tradition of magic mirrors, fantasy reflects not only ourselves and our shadows, but the truth of our hearts.

I think this is one of the reasons some people fear fantasy.

Author of Talking to Dragons, Mairelon the Magician, The Seven Towers . . .

Geoff Ryman

GEE, I HOPE I LIKE THIS PICTURE.

I haven't seen it yet, so you are seeing it, effectively, at the same time I am. This is just as well. I hate pictures of myself. I've only just gotten used to how old and haggard I looked back in 1989. Every new photo taken since 1989 is a shock. Then people explain how much younger it makes me look.

Being photographed as an author is strange. It is next to impossible to meet the person who writes the book; you just meet their less interesting twin who negotiates the real world. What you get in a photograph is the less interesting twin trying to look the part of the person who really writes the books, but who is not available just now to take the call. The author has always just stepped out, and will always be back at his or her desk in just a moment.

Would you like to leave a message?

Gee, I wish my books were still in print.

Author of Was, Unconquered Country, The Child Garden . . .

Elyse Guttenberg

I WRITE FROM A SENSE OF PLACE, primarily Alaskan and primarily wilderness. I hadn't realized this for a long time, not intellectually. It was halfway through my first fantasy novel *Sunder, Eclipse and Seed* that I noticed how the details of a northern environment had begun first to accumulate, and then to interact with the story.

It isn't simply setting I'm talking about, nor only one type of landscape that interests me; picturesque vistas can be found by following most any road. But there is a belief I've come to as a writer that stories and characters have the most depth when they open doors and step outside of cars and houses and walk in a place where the land itself challenges, where it reminds them constantly who they are, what they need to be doing.

No, I'm not recommending that we all write survival stories, nor would I want to think that my characters will routinely find themselves struggling along on mountaintops, coasts, or river gorges.

But in Alaska I have found a place where people spend a good deal of effort puzzling over how to survive, not in spite of the land but because of it, and it's a discovery I feel fortunate to have made. It's given me stories and a way of life I thrive on, a place where building codes are few enough that my husband and I were able to build our house completely by ourselves. It's a place where, when I need a break from the long hours of sitting at my desk, I chop firewood or go for long walks at temperatures often colder than –20°F along a road that in deep winter isn't touched by daylight until noon, in summer doesn't see a hint of dark for months.

Does every writer need to live near wilderness to write meaningfully? I don't believe so. I'm also a product of another environment: New York City, where I grew up. It's a place I had to leave before I could appreciate how rich were its voices, how varied and filled with history. Have I just contradicted myself? I don't think so. Characters in stories, people in real life—we react to the landscape around us in as many different ways as there are languages and dialects in the world, and all offer meaning. It's my hope that as a writer, I'll continue to take my characters out of their cabins, or apartments, and put them on the streets, or rural backwaters, and let them find out who we are.

Author of Sunder, Eclipse and Seed; Summer Light; The House in the Moon . . .

Tracy Hickman

I BELIEVE THAT THE REAL VALUE and meaning in any story is found only in the white space between the words. The human mind demands closure: My description of a character—words on the page—only vaguely outlines that creation in clay. It is the reader's mind that breathes life in the character—life provided by the reader's own imagination.

That's the wonder of books. Books are the first and best interactive media. Books are interactive? Absolutely! As a storyteller, I see my job as a conjurer, summoning up images from the reader's mind. The reader interacts with the text to create a vision more complete and personal than in any other entertainment form.

The truth is that I just love to tell stories and have been blessed by God with the wonderful people who showed me how to tell them well.

Most of my books have been coauthored with Margaret Weis. She's always had top billing between us and with good reason: While I could dream up the story, she knew how to *tell* it and share it with others. She has been my coauthor, business associate, friend, and mentor.

None of this would have happened if it hadn't been for my wife, Laura. She always picked me up when I fell down, told me I could do it and shoved me back into the game.

Ah, so many stories—so little time to tell them all!

Author (with Margaret Weis) of *The Dragon Lance Chronicles, The Deathgate Cycle,* The Darksword trilogy . . .

Lisa Goldstein

IT DOESN'T LOOK LIKE IT TO MOST PEOPLE, but in the opinion of their friends my parents had a sort of mixed marriage. My mother was a Hungarian Jew, like Harry Houdini and Peter Lorre and Frida Kahlo's father. (Houdini even had the same last name—Weiss—as my grandmother. I'd like to believe that we're related, but it was, unfortunately, too common a name.) Jews from Eastern Europe tended to be mystics: They danced to become closer to God, they added and subtracted the numerical values of letters to find the meanings hidden in the world. My father, on the other hand, was a German Jew, like Marx and Freud and Einstein, logical, rational, interested in scientific connections.

I've always wondered why it's the same people who like the impossibilities of fantasy and the rigorous constructions of science fiction, why they will happily go from Tolkien to Arthur C. Clarke and back again. In my own case, though, this contradiction (if it is one) seems to have been there since I was born.

Author of *The Red Magician, Strange Devices of the Sun and Moon, Tourists* . . .

Lynn Abbey

MAGIC.

It took contemporary technological magic to slice time thin enough to capture me.

I can be quiet and still, but not my hands. My hands are rarely frozen, empty, at rest.

I am what I've done and what I do: raising stepchildren, writing books, embroidering with cotton, silk, and wool. My imagination is fueled by motion, not repose: I get my best ideas when I'm rearranging the furniture.

Whether it's rafting in the Grand Canyon, exploring an eleventh-century castle in Normandy, or guiding characters through a fantasy world, my hands tell my story. They're braver than the rest of me and filled with confidence.

I go where they take me.

Author of *The Black Flame, Beneath the Web, Siege of Shadows...*

Gene Wolfe

FANTASY IS THE EASIEST THING TO WRITE, and one of the hardest to write well. It is hard because good fantasy, like good art, demands that we depict what we see.

And not what we "know" to be "true." I once put a witch and a private detective in the same book, and I have been told ever since that I am not to do that by people who will not see that the private detective and the witch often live in the same block.

The universe is extensive, and time wider than any sea; it is our good fortune, Horatio, to live at a time and in a place vastly richer than most in those things that are not to be found in your philosophy.

My editor says, and says truly, that he has become the man he wanted to be as a child. I, too, have been fortunate. As a child I wanted very badly to have adventures and go to Oz. I have had many and look forward to more; and on the tenth or it may have been the twentieth occasion that I watched Bert Lahr rescue Judy Garland from the pigs (the newspaper I read every day does not even know that pigs are dangerous) I realized that I was born here: Kansas is black-and-white, and that's not where I live.

Not so long ago I saw a magnificent German shepherd lunge from between two parked cars, held in check by a blonde who could have played first base in the National League. And it struck me that a fantastic adventure could have been filmed on the spot simply by hanging a skull about that woman's neck and equipping her with a broadsword—but the woman and her dog are everything, while the skull and the sword are nothing.

Fantasy is life seen whole, and reading fantasy enables us to do it. (I will not say "*only* life seen whole," because life includes all that is and is not.) We have heroes and heroines, castles and curses, seers and sorcerers, angels and alchemists, and invisible airplanes. We have that woman and her dog and a million more wonders, and all that is necessary for fantasy is a visitor from Kansas.

Author of The Book of the New Sun, Soldier of the Mist, Calde of the Long Sun . . .

Diana Paxson

I BELIEVE THAT MAGIC IS REAL. . . .

I also believe that reality is magical—just as strange and significant and serendipitous, and as luminous with the power of spirit, as any vision of fantasy translated onto a page. This does not result in what is usually called "magical realism," which has always struck me as being more "surreal," but in something else. Perhaps "hard fantasy" would be a more useful description. The real work of magic is done in the head, not with a magic wand, and the act of writing fiction uses the mind in much the same way.

Magic, like writing, is most successful when it appears effortless and free. But in both cases, the freedom is the result of practice, experience, and informed adherence to the principles of the craft. I will not call them Laws or Rules, which seem to me too mechanical, and in any case can be broken if you know what you are doing. The function of principles is to guide.

The concept of principle is relevant to fantasy in another way as well.

If you reread the old fairy tales, you will notice a very strict etiquette. In an expanded context, fantasy is the same. If science fiction proclaims itself the "literature of ideas," then fantasy might be called the "literature of ethics." These days we have gotten away from the dualistic insistence that characters be all-bad or all-good, but the foundation of a good fantasy is the conflict between good and evil *forces*. In fantasy, you can not only tell the difference between them, but it makes a difference which you choose.

In historical fantasy, which has been my major focus for the past few years, the problem is complicated by the fact that the story is taking place in our own world, and I am sure that people who lived in other times were as confused about what was going on as we are today. In the old epics, the hero often dies, and this is not considered tragic, but a victory, because he knows what he is fighting *for*, and his death serves a purpose. In writing a historical fantasy, I try to find some pattern in the confusion of my characters' lives.

At the social and historical levels, this is the same as looking for the magic in the "real" world. It is the nature—perhaps the function—of humans to try to *understand* their experience of the world. The sense of wonder is awakened by realizing that all the traumas actually make sense, and that the world is not a dull, mechanical place at all, but full of magic and meaning.

Author of The Wolf and the Raven, The Dragons of the Rhine, The Lord of Horses . . .

Garry Kilworth

IF I WANTED TO KNOW where my ideas came from I wouldn't be an imaginative writer, I'd be a scientist. My whole life has been spent daydreaming and out of those daydreams come stories. It doesn't interest me where daydreams come from, what interests me is helping them grow and blossom into something different, some strange and wonderful tale of mystery and magic. Then again, if you asked a few scientists where they got their ideas from they might tell you they spent most of their life daydreaming and out of those daydreams came something different, some strange and wonderful discovery or invention. It could be that a scientist and storyteller might nourish the same daydream, one growing into a fabulous tale, the other into a marvelous machine—one fantastical, the other real.

Author of *Hunter's Moon: A Story of Foxes, Witchwater Country, Dark Hills, Hollow Clocks* . . .

Gordon R. Dickson

HUMAN BEINGS HAVE TO BE what they are and do what they must.

But when a good storyteller places those human beings in a situation never before encountered, or even suspected to exist—then from a unique and different angle, light is reflected onto the human condition.

In the final essential, the telling of a story is the highest of the arts of literature. Only if a story is first and foremost compelling, *as a story*, can there be room for something more; so that in classic literature we find the stories of action and adventure that are so well told that they have room to reflect light upon some real and important element in a human individual or human society.

Author of The Dragon and the George, The Dragon Knight, The Dragon on the Border . . .

Madeleine L'Engle

ONE DAY A RENOWNED CLOCK-MAKER and repairer came through the village, and the people crowded around him and begged him to fix their broken clocks and watches. He spent many hours looking at all the faulty time pieces, and at last he announced that he could repair only those whose owners had kept them wound, because they were the only ones which would be able to remember how to keep time.

So we must daily keep things wound: that is, we must pray when prayer seems dry as dust; we must write when we are physically tired, when our hearts are heavy, when our bodies are in pain.

We may not always be able to make our "clock" run correctly, but at least we can keep it wound, so that it will not forget.

From the chapter "Keeping the Clock Wound," *Walking on Water*, Harold Shaw Publishers.
Author of *A Wrinkle in Time, A Wind in the Door, A Swiftly Tilting Planet . . .*

Terry Brooks

FANTASY PROVIDES ME with a different way of looking at reality. My longtime editor, Lester del Rey, used to argue that fantasy was the most difficult form of literature to write because it had to be the most realistic. What he meant was that if the reader couldn't suspend disbelief long enough to accept the possibility of the story, then the writer had failed. I've come to believe he was right in his assessment. Most of what I write is, metaphorically, about our own world. The plots that make up the particulars of my stories are almost always inspired by what I read in the newspapers. By putting the story in a different world, I can take a fresh look at the particulars and perhaps bring to the reader a different perspective. My first goal is to tell a good story, but my second is to make the readers think about their own lives.

Author of *The Sword of Shannara, The Black Unicorn, The Tangle Box* . . .

Katherine Kurtz

IF ANY ONE THEME PERMEATES the first quarter-century of my writing, it's probably the whole question of differences—of whether "different" is necessarily wrong or bad—in short, the nature and possible consequences of blind prejudice, not based in facts. A fantasy perspective can reduce the immediacy of any threat such examination might present to the reader—after all, it isn't "real"—but new seeds are planted. Or maybe the process stirs up material already in the reader's mind. Or maybe a little of both.

In this regard, I like to return to my training as a chemist and think of myself as a catalyst. I don't participate directly in the process—after all, I'm not even there while the reader reads—but I provide the conditions under which changes in thinking can take place. I don't presume to change minds—but I do hope to open a few . . .

Author of Deryni Rising, Camber of Culdi, The King's Justice . . .

Stephen R. Lawhead

I BELIEVE IN THE POWER OF MYTH to inform our lives and illuminate our common path. Unfortunately, the myths we receive at long remove are often so sullied and shopworn that their power has ceased to flow. As a writer, I find I spend considerable time and effort in trying to rescue the mythic spirit of the stories I tell, and then restore both shape and substance to their rightful prominence so that the myth's inherent power can flow again. This has been my primary interest in pursuing the Matter of Britain through the five novels of *The Pendragon Cycle*, and in *The Song of Albion Trilogy*.

I am sometimes asked why I insist on adding a spiritual dimension to my tales. I say that I am merely putting back the element others so often leave out—through ignorance, weakness, or deliberate fault.

The myths and legends of long ago are meant to show us who we are and what we may become, and to point out the pitfalls along the way to our final destination. We are travelers on a spiritual journey. There are guides and spirits along the way to befriend us—if our eyes are open and our hearts are willing.

Author of *The Pendragon Cycle*, *The Song of Albion Trilogy*, and the Dragon King trilogy

217

Esther M. Friesner

NO ONE IS IN A POSITION to second-guess history, but I have the feeling that if I am remembered for any one aspect of my writing it will be for the "funny stuff." This is just fine with me. In a world often painful and still more frequently ludicrous, laughter is the great comforter and healer. It has the power to make us feel better about the human condition, but it also has the power to make us think, to force us to reevaluate certain cultural givens, to recognize long-standing, long-enduring social wrongs and—I hope—to correct them.

Humor has power, which accounts for how much some people fear it and how energetically they dismiss it as mere foolery. They find it convenient to forget that the kings of old kept court fools as much for their wisdom and insight as for their jokes and caperings.

Given that, I'll be more than happy and proud to be remembered for the laughter.

Of course, if I'm remembered for some other facet of my work, I guess the joke's on me.

Author of *Yesterday We Saw Mermaids, Witchwood Cradle, Harpy High . . .*

Jane Fancher

WHEN PATTI SAID, "LET'S TRY THE STAIRCASE," my first thought was: But what about my stuff? My books? The koi pond? My second was: Patti's the artist, it's her book, so shut up and cooperate.

Evidently, Patti knew what she wanted; a few shots with available light, and we were done.

Later, in that hazy realm between waking and sleep where so many truths come clear, I had my third (relevant) thought: My stories don't come from my stuff, or from research books . . . not even from my koi pond. All my research, all my personal experiences, all my insights and extrapolations become a story through a unique, constantly metamorphosing sieve: me.

Disturbing realization.

And (I thought) here in the bedroom at the top of that very staircase is where I first encounter the heart and soul of my stories: the characters. (Apparently they live in that aforementioned sleep/waking threshold.) Down the stairs and to the left are my computer and research books, source of the stories' bone and muscle, flesh and color. To the right is the Outside, where every writer's collaborators, the readers, live. They give the stories purpose.

So where, I asked myself as I lay awake in the dark, does the magic fit in? Where, the technological marvels of science fiction? And I realized those elements are the unique mirrors I use to reflect humanity at a slightly different perspective, angled just enough to help us face truths that might otherwise be too painfully personal to acknowledge, or too far beyond personal experience to comprehend. By vicariously confronting those truths, not with magic or techno-toys, but with very real, very human strengths, we learn to be a tad less suspicious, a touch less frightened, a little less ashamed—and a bit more excited about our own possibilities.

Deciding the realization wasn't so disturbing after all, I stepped across the threshold.

Author of Groundties, Uplink, Gate of Ivrel: Claiming Rites . . .

Chelsea Quinn Yarbro

NOT TO PUT TOO FINE A POINT ON IT, high fantasy does not often hold my interest. *Low* fantasy, on the other hand, intrigues the hell out of me. And I assume that my readers will like better those stories I am stimulated by more than those done out of craft alone. I am particularly enthusiastic about juxtaposing creatures out of legend/myth with the real world, if possible turning the mythic figure upside-down, inside-out, or back-to-front in the process, as should be apparent in my various historical horror novels. I also enjoy extrapolating imaginary constructs in new, real-world-based environments, as was the case in *Ariosto*. That does not mean I would want to limit myself to the fantasy genre without ventures into other writing arenas; I got used to genre-hopping more than twenty years ago and by now it's a habit.

As to why I do it: I write because I cannot imagine — and I have a vivid imagination — doing anything else (except compose music).

Author of the Saint-Germain sequence, Ogilvie, Tallant & Moon series, Atta Olivia Clemens books . . .

Barbara Hambly

FOR ME, writing is a way to defeat and circumvent Time. I was trained as a historian—I love doing period pieces, both fantasies and murder mysteries, because the research is a form of time travel, a way of seeing places as they were before I was born. And on another level, writing is a way of reaching into the time-stream of my own life and crystallizing things that I want to keep forever: what someone I love looked like when we were teenagers, or the shade and cool of old hiking trails that have been buried under housing developments now for the past twenty years.

I have a sort of locker-room, or Characters' Lounge, in the back of my head—some of those people in there, I've been telling stories about since I was twelve. When I get an idea for a story I'll do a casting call, and see who suits up and comes out.

I'm the only person I know who knew from the age of four what she wanted to be when she grew up. Writing is my hobby as well as my living—now and then I'll still write novel-length stories that I know are unpublishable for legal reasons, just because the story amuses me. Everybody told me I couldn't make a living as a writer, and I spent years trying to figure out what I *could* make a living at that would let me be a writer on the side. I'm glad they were wrong.

Author of *Those Who Hunt the Night*, the Windrose series, *Bride of the Rat God*...

224

Dennis L. McKiernan

I HAVE ALWAYS KNOWN that a story gets its *energy* from conflict, challenge, peril, but what I didn't fully realize until I started writing was that a tale gets its *substance* from the philosophy embedded within. Just as energy and matter make up the vital essence of the universe, so too do challenge and philosophy constitute the essential marrow of a tale . . . and if one or the other of these crucial factors is missing, then the result is a "universe" half-formed. Like Yin and Yang, energy and substance drive one another—challenge arising from underlying truths, truths discovered as a consequence of challenge, fundamental questions deriving from both. It is a joy to find energy *and* substance in a gifted story, for each is a precious jewel with a fully formed universe inside.

Author of *The Eye of the Hunter, Dragondoom, Caverns of Socrates* . . .

Tim Powers

FROM THE TIME I WAS ELEVEN until the time I was twenty, I read every bit of science fiction and fantasy I could get my hands on. After that I read more widely, and of the perhaps hundred books I read in a year nowadays, probably not even six are SF or fantasy—but the deeply imprinted notion of *story* I absorbed during those uncritical early years remains my rock-bottom foundation, and I'm sure that if I live to be a hundred I won't ever have been able to conceive of a plot that didn't involve something like vampires or time travel or orbiting colonies or pictures in old photo albums that come to life and sing offensive songs in the middle of the night.

Most of what I write is fantasy, which is even more handicapped, in the eyes of the world at large, than strict science fiction is; after all, at least the events in a science fiction story *could* happen, while the trappings of fantasy—ghosts, talking animals, magic rings, old gods who really are old gods—are obviously, totally bogus. I'm convinced that this requires fantasy stories to be even more plausible on a surface level, a tactile and sensory and real-world level, than "mainstream" fiction. So maybe all the reading I've done since twenty has not been entirely without value.

Author of The Anubis Gates, Closing Time, Expiration Date . . .

Index

The Faces of Fantasy

Designed by Michael Mendelsohn

Art direction by Irene Gallo

Composed at MM Design 2000, Inc., in

Sabon on the Power Macintosh 7500

using QuarkXPress

Printed by Butler & Tanner Ltd.,

Frome, Somerset, England, on

80 lb. Precision Smooth

Bound by Butler & Tanner Ltd.

PATTI PERRET studied photography in the fine arts department at Indiana University. She moved to New York City, where she assisted internationally renowned photojournalist Mary Ellen Mark. She also worked for Woody Allen on the films *Stardust Memories* and *A Midsummer Night's Sex Comedy*.

Her professional credits also include work as the staff photographer for *Saturday Night Live*, where she created the opening montage and shot portraits of the hosts and bands; feature film production stills and marquee posters; CD and album covers; and magazine photographs for publications around the world. She lives in New Orleans with her husband and two sons.

TERRI WINDLING is an author, artist, and editor who has worked in the fantasy field for more than fifteen years. Winner of five World Fantasy Awards, she is the coeditor of *The Year's Best Fantasy and Horror* and a consulting editor for Tor Books. She lives in Tucson, Arizona, and Devon, England.